This Book Belongs To:

The Truce of God

"Softly," he said···"No harsh words."

The Truce of God
By Mary Roberts Rinehart

Decorations by Harold Sichel

Watchmaker Publishing
1929

Chapter One

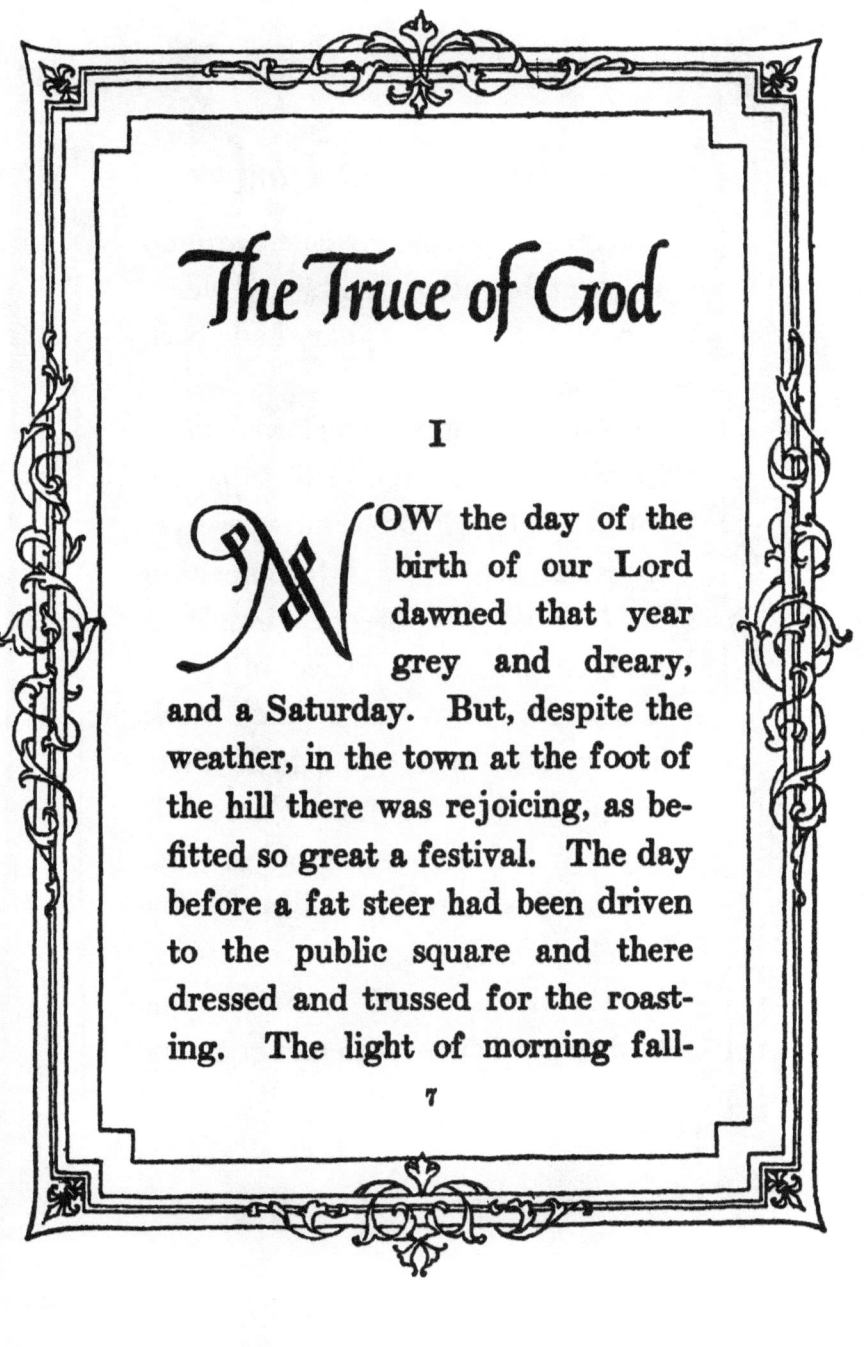

The Truce of God

I

NOW the day of the birth of our Lord dawned that year grey and dreary, and a Saturday. But, despite the weather, in the town at the foot of the hill there was rejoicing, as befitted so great a festival. The day before a fat steer had been driven to the public square and there dressed and trussed for the roasting. The light of morning fall-

7

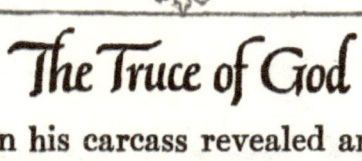

The Truce of God

ing on his carcass revealed around it great heaps of fruits and vege-tables. For the year had been prosperous.

But the young overlord sulked in his castle at the cliff top, and bit his nails. From Thursday eve-ning of each week to the morning of Monday, Mother Church had decreed peace, a Truce of God. Three full days out of each week his men-at-arms polished their weapons and grew fat. Three full days out of each week his grudge against his cousin, Philip of the Black Beard, must feed on itself.

His dark mood irritated the Bishop of Tours, who had come to

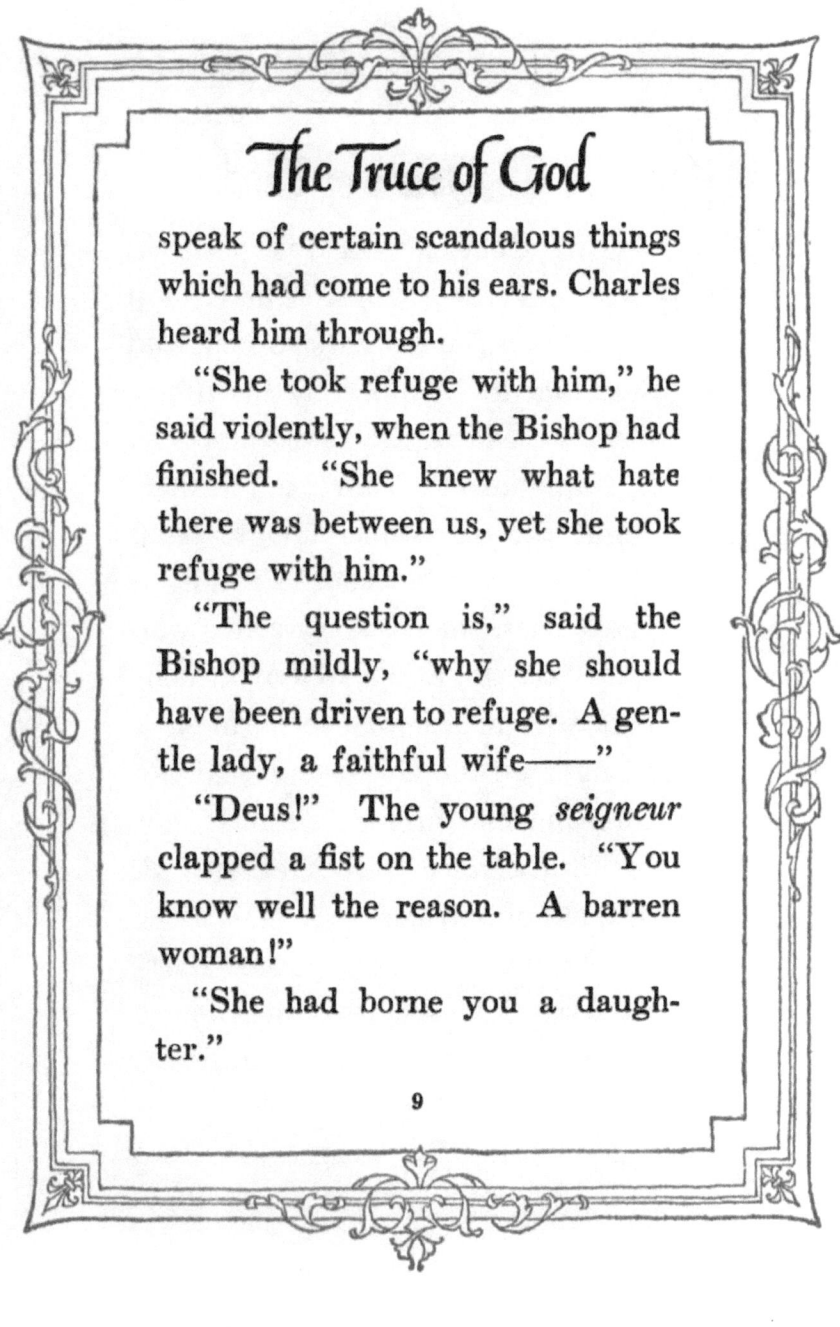

The Truce of God

speak of certain scandalous things which had come to his ears. Charles heard him through.

"She took refuge with him," he said violently, when the Bishop had finished. "She knew what hate there was between us, yet she took refuge with him."

"The question is," said the Bishop mildly, "why she should have been driven to refuge. A gentle lady, a faithful wife——"

"Deus!" The young *seigneur* clapped a fist on the table. "You know well the reason. A barren woman!"

"She had borne you a daughter."

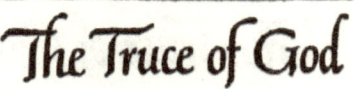

The Truce of God

But Charles was far gone in rage and out of hand. The Bishop took his offended ears to bed, and left him to sit alone by the dying fire, with bitterness for company.

Came into the courtyard at midnight the Christmas singers from the town; the blacksmith rolling a great bass, the crockery-seller who sang falsetto, and a fool of the village who had slept overnight in a manger on the holy eve a year before and had brought from it, not wit, but a voice from Heaven. A miracle of miracles.

The men-at-arms in the courtyard stood back to give them space. They sang with eyes upturned,

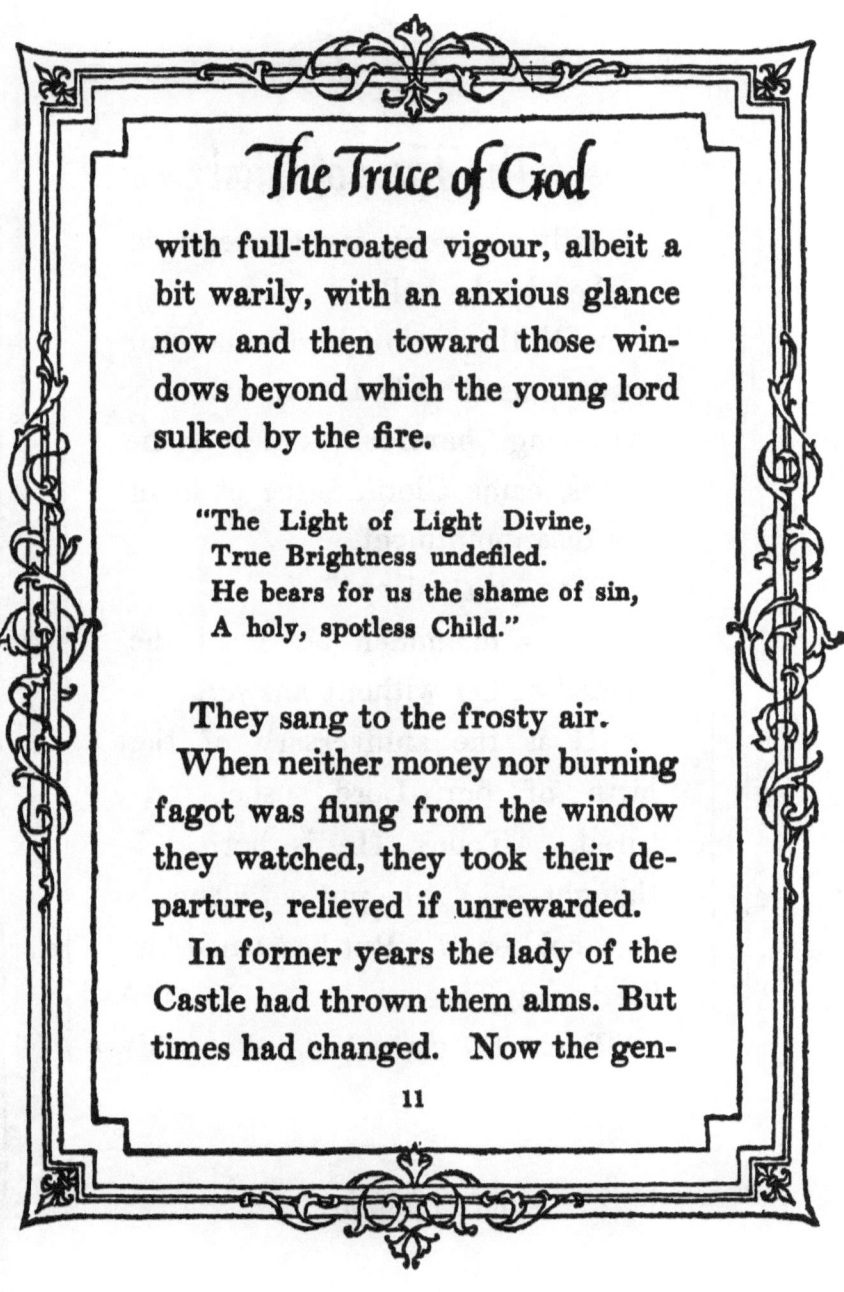

The Truce of God

with full-throated vigour, albeit a bit warily, with an anxious glance now and then toward those windows beyond which the young lord sulked by the fire.

> "The Light of Light Divine,
> True Brightness undefiled.
> He bears for us the shame of sin,
> A holy, spotless Child."

They sang to the frosty air.

When neither money nor burning fagot was flung from the window they watched, they took their departure, relieved if unrewarded.

In former years the lady of the Castle had thrown them alms. But times had changed. Now the gen-

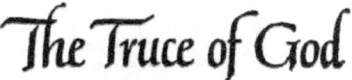

The Truce of God

tle lady was gone, and the *seigneur* sulked in the hall.

With the dawn Charles the Fair took himself to bed. And to him, pattering barefoot along stone floors, came Clotilde, the child of his disappointment.

"Are you asleep?"

One arm under his head, he looked at her without answer.

"It is the anniversary of the birth of our Lord," she ventured. "Today He is born. I thought——" She put out a small, very cold hand. But he turned his head away.

"Back to your bed," he said

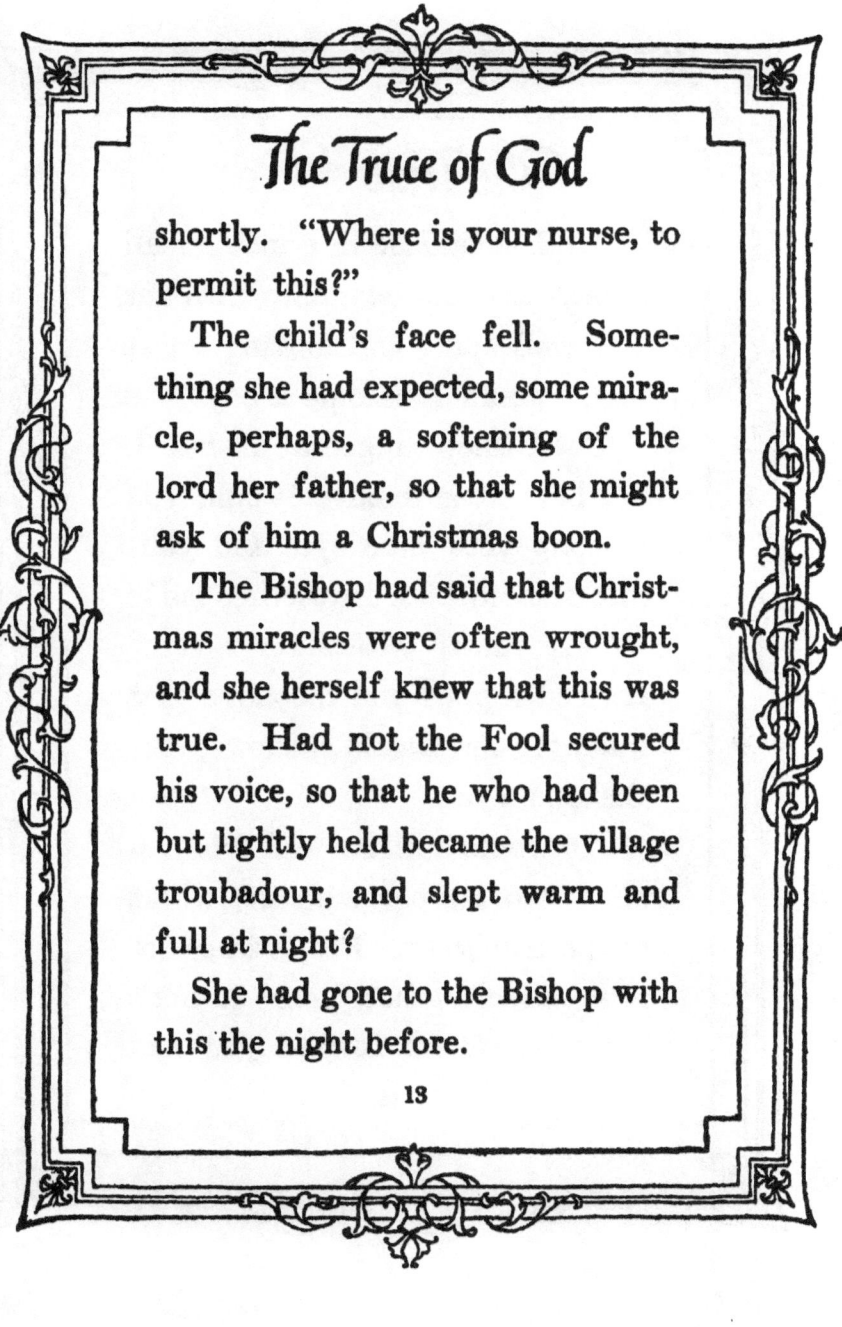

shortly. "Where is your nurse, to permit this?"

The child's face fell. Something she had expected, some miracle, perhaps, a softening of the lord her father, so that she might ask of him a Christmas boon.

The Bishop had said that Christmas miracles were often wrought, and she herself knew that this was true. Had not the Fool secured his voice, so that he who had been but lightly held became the village troubadour, and slept warm and full at night?

She had gone to the Bishop with this the night before.

13

The Truce of God

"If I should lie in a manger all night," she said, standing with her feet well apart and looking up at him, "would I become a boy?"

The Bishop tugged at his beard. "A boy, little maid! Would you give up your blue eyes and your soft skin to be a roystering lad?"

"My father wishes for a son," she had replied and the cloud that was over the Castle shadowed the Bishop's eyes.

"It would not be well," he replied, "to tamper with the works of the Almighty. Pray rather for this miracle, that your father's heart be turned toward you and

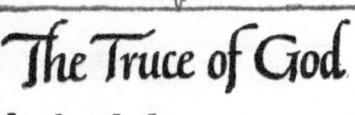

The Truce of God

toward the lady, your mother."

So during much of the night she had asked this boon steadfastly. But clearly she had not been heard.

"Back to your bed!" said her father, and turned his face away.

So she went as far as the leather curtain which hung in the doorway and there she turned.

"Why do they sing?" she had asked the Bishop, of the blacksmith and the others, and he had replied into his beard, "To soften the hard of heart."

So she turned in the doorway and sang in her reedy little voice, much thinned by the cold, sang to soften her young father's heart.

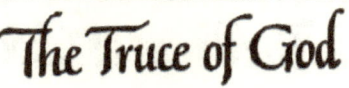

The Truce of God

"The Light of Light Divine,
True Brightness undefiled.
He bears for us the shame of sin,
A holy, spotless Child."

But the song failed. Perhaps it was the wrong hour, or perhaps it was because she had not slept in the manger and brought forth the gift of voice.

"Blood of the martyrs!" shouted her father, and raised himself on his elbow. "Are you mad? Get back to your bed. I shall have a word with someone for this."

Whether it had softened him or not it had stirred him, so she made her plea.

"It is His birthday. I want to see my mother."

16

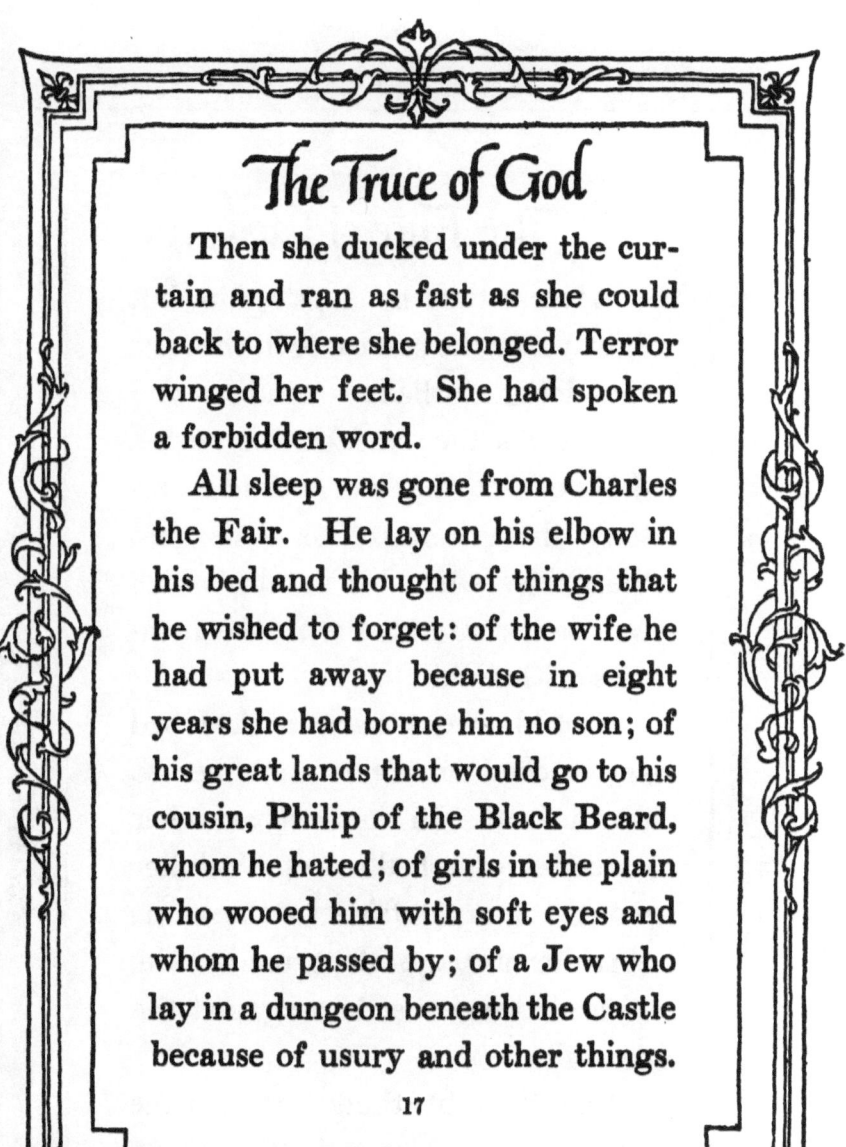

The Truce of God

Then she ducked under the curtain and ran as fast as she could back to where she belonged. Terror winged her feet. She had spoken a forbidden word.

All sleep was gone from Charles the Fair. He lay on his elbow in his bed and thought of things that he wished to forget: of the wife he had put away because in eight years she had borne him no son; of his great lands that would go to his cousin, Philip of the Black Beard, whom he hated; of girls in the plain who wooed him with soft eyes and whom he passed by; of a Jew who lay in a dungeon beneath the Castle because of usury and other things.

The Truce of God

After a time he slept again, but lightly, for the sun came in through the deep, unshaded window and fell on his face and on the rushes that covered the floor. And in his sleep the grimness was gone, and the pride. And his mouth, which was sad, contended with the firmness of his chin.

Clotilde went back to her bed and tucked her feet under her to warm them. In the next room her nurse lay on a bed asleep, with her mouth open; outside in the stone corridor a page slept on a skin, with a corner over him against the draught.

She thought things over while

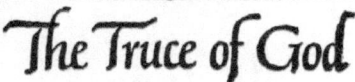

The Truce of God

she warmed her feet. It was clear that singing did not soften all hearts. Perhaps she did not sing very well. But the Bishop had said that after one had done a good act one might pray with hope. She decided to do a good act and then to pray to see her mother; she would pray also to become a boy so that her father might care for her. But the Bishop considered it a little late for such a prayer.

She made terms with the Almighty, sitting on her bed.

"I shall do a good act," she said, "on this the birthday of Thy Son, and after that I shall ask for the thing Thou knowest of."

19

The Truce of God

After much thinking, she decided to free the Jew. And being, after all, her father's own child, she acted at once.

It was a matter of many cold stone steps and much fumbling with bars. But Guillem the gaoler had crept up to the hall and lay sleeping by the fire, with a dozen dogs about him. It was the time of the Truce of God, and vigilance was relaxed. Also Guillem was in love with a girl of the village and there was talk that the *seigneur,* in his loneliness, had seen that she was beautiful. So Guillem slept to forget, and the Jew

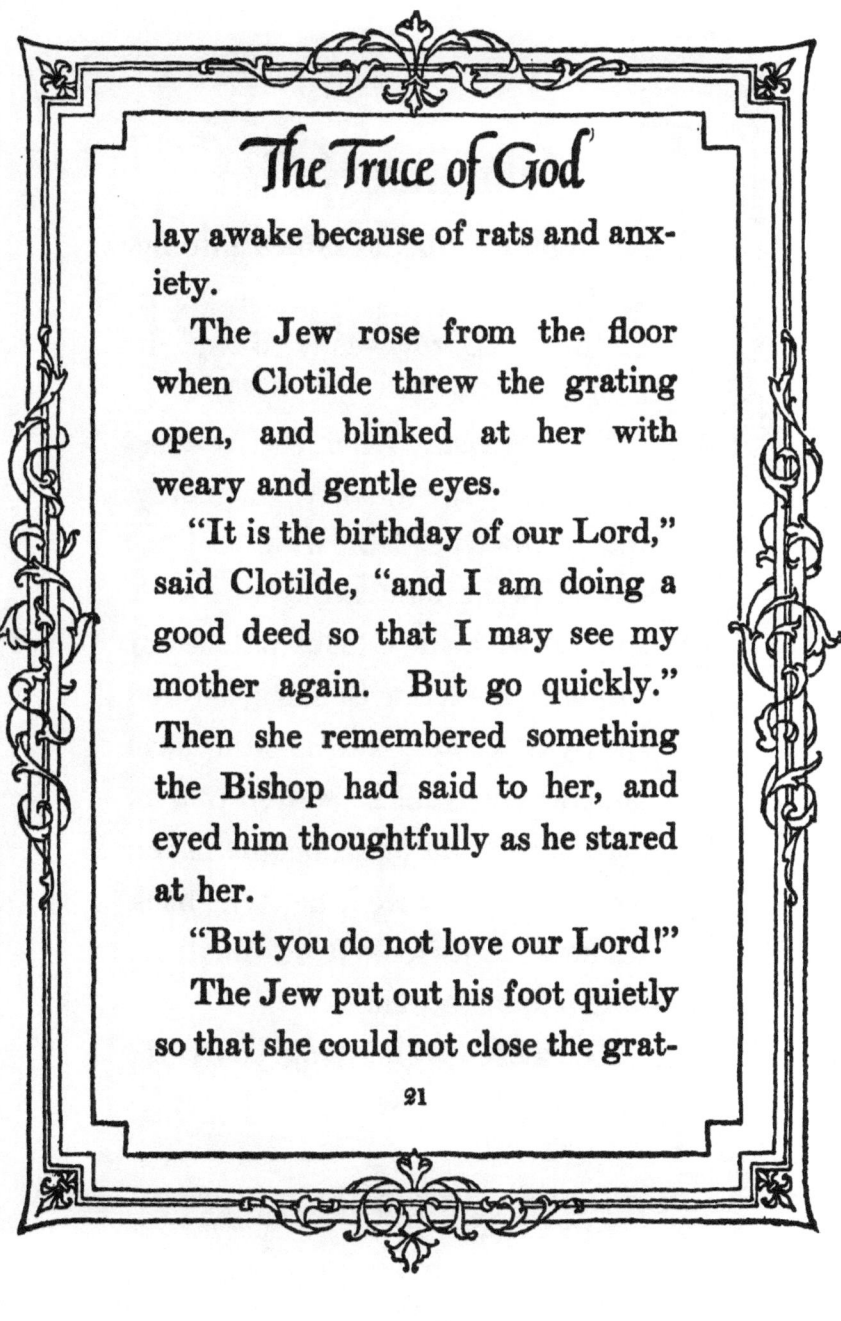

The Truce of God

lay awake because of rats and anxiety.

The Jew rose from the floor when Clotilde threw the grating open, and blinked at her with weary and gentle eyes.

"It is the birthday of our Lord," said Clotilde, "and I am doing a good deed so that I may see my mother again. But go quickly." Then she remembered something the Bishop had said to her, and eyed him thoughtfully as he stared at her.

"But you do not love our Lord!"

The Jew put out his foot quietly so that she could not close the grat-

21

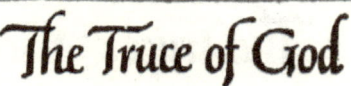

ing again. But he smiled into her eyes.

"Your Lord was a Jew," he said.

This reassured her. It seemed to double the quality of mercy. She threw the door wide and the usurer went out cautiously, as if suspecting a trap. But patches of sunlight, barred with black, showed the way clear. He should have gone at once, but he waited to give her the blessing of his people. Even then, having started, he went back to her. She looked so small in that fearsome place.

"If there is something you wish,

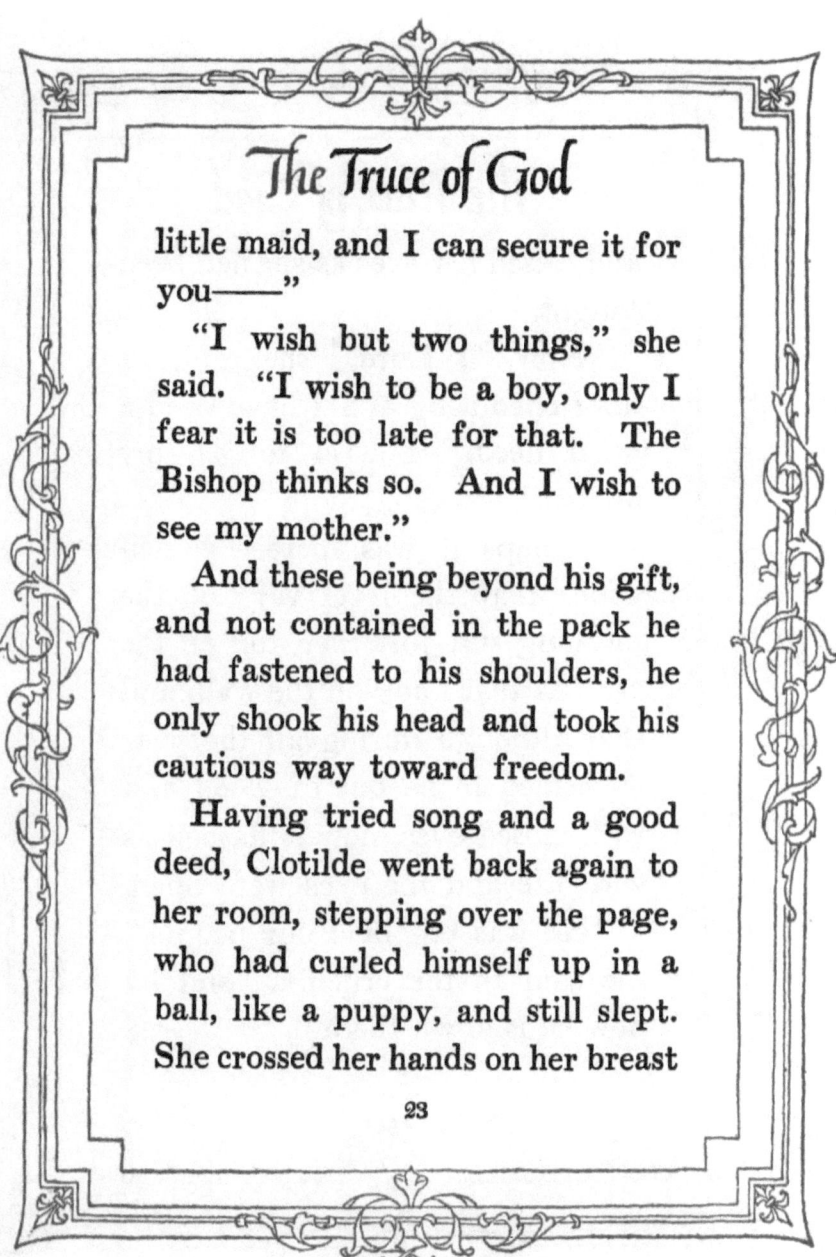

little maid, and I can secure it for you——"

"I wish but two things," she said. "I wish to be a boy, only I fear it is too late for that. The Bishop thinks so. And I wish to see my mother."

And these being beyond his gift, and not contained in the pack he had fastened to his shoulders, he only shook his head and took his cautious way toward freedom.

Having tried song and a good deed, Clotilde went back again to her room, stepping over the page, who had curled himself up in a ball, like a puppy, and still slept. She crossed her hands on her breast

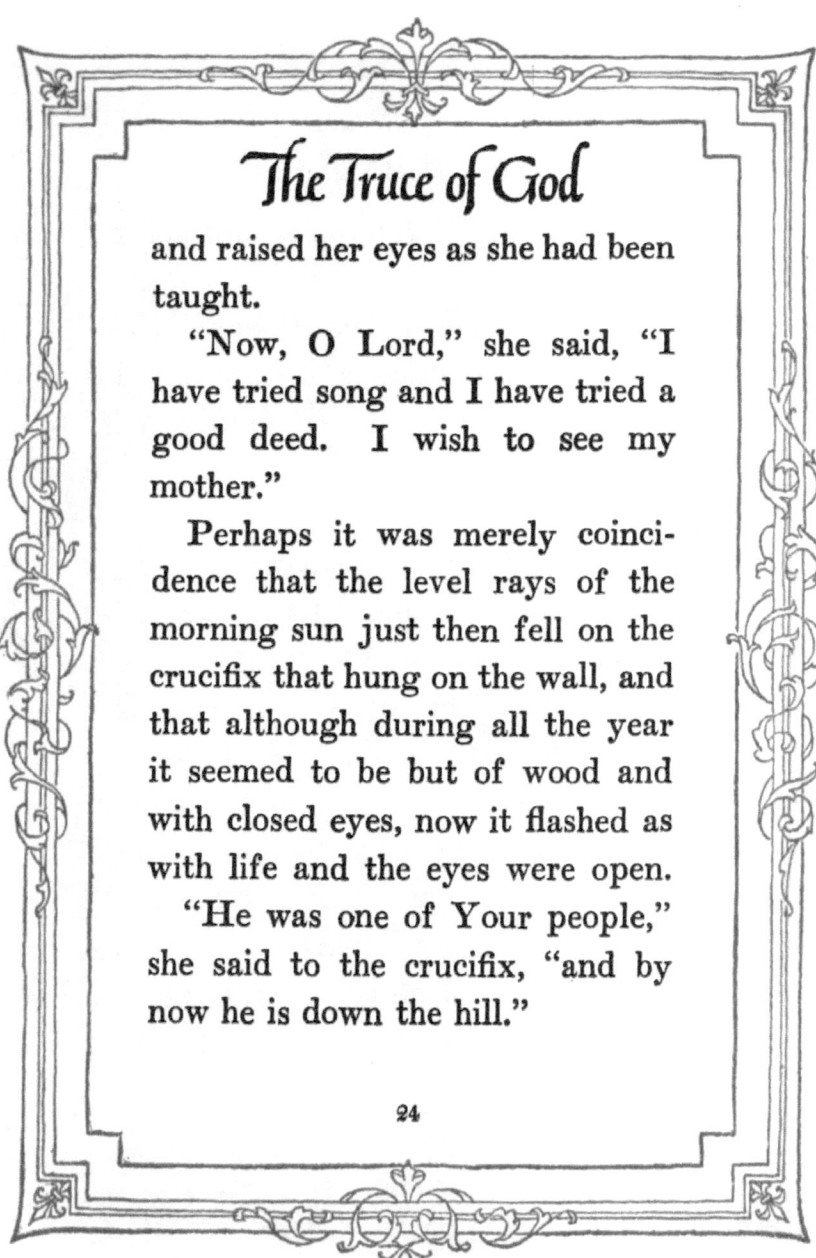

The Truce of God

and raised her eyes as she had been taught.

"Now, O Lord," she said, "I have tried song and I have tried a good deed. I wish to see my mother."

Perhaps it was merely coincidence that the level rays of the morning sun just then fell on the crucifix that hung on the wall, and that although during all the year it seemed to be but of wood and with closed eyes, now it flashed as with life and the eyes were open.

"He was one of Your people," she said to the crucifix, "and by now he is down the hill."

Chapter Two

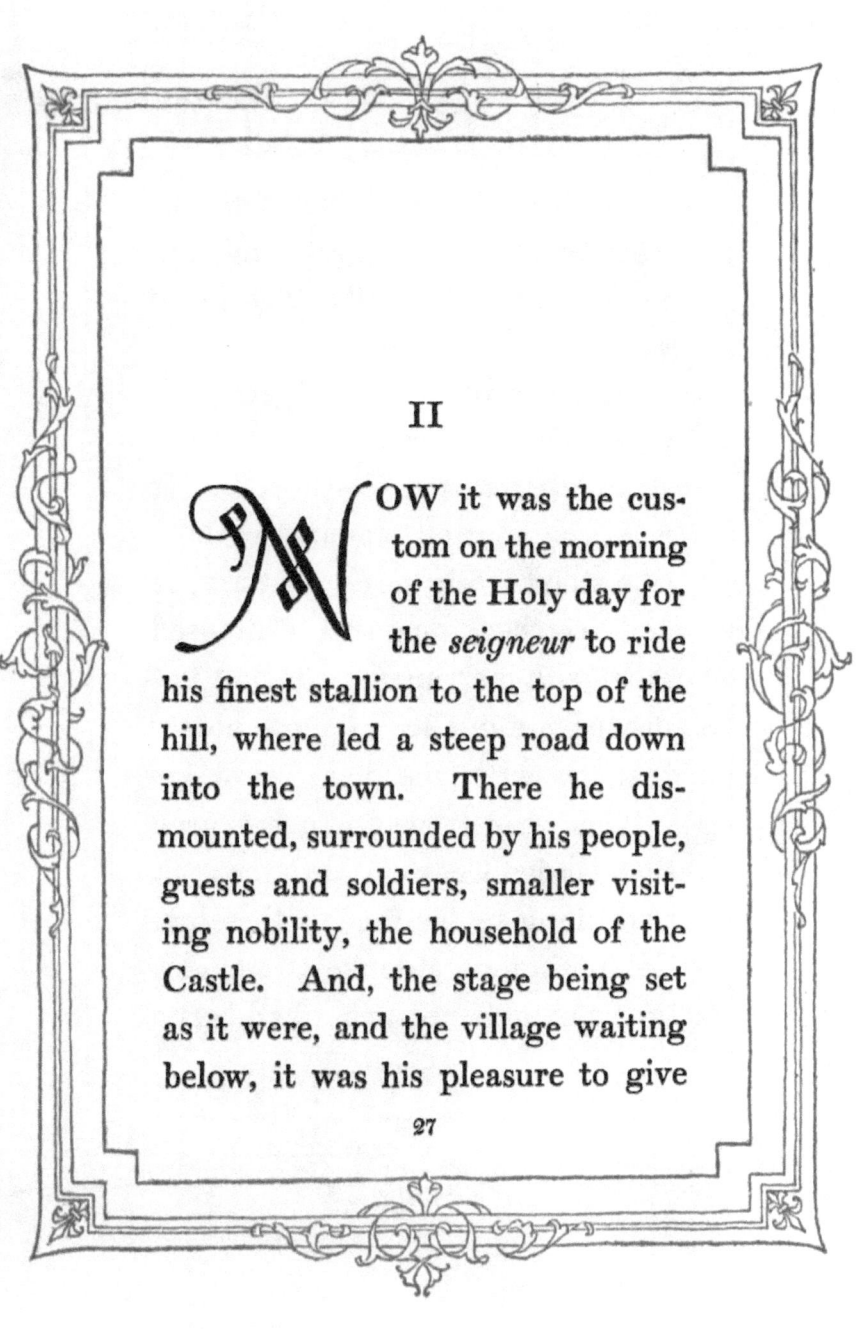

II

NOW it was the custom on the morning of the Holy day for the *seigneur* to ride his finest stallion to the top of the hill, where led a steep road down into the town. There he dismounted, surrounded by his people, guests and soldiers, smaller visiting nobility, the household of the Castle. And, the stage being set as it were, and the village waiting below, it was his pleasure to give his charger a great cut with the whip and send him galloping, un-ridden, down the hill. The horse was his who caught it.

Below waited the villagers, di-vided between terror and cupidity. Above waited the Castle folk. It was an amusing game for those who stood safely along the parapet and watched, one that convulsed them with merriment. Also, it im-proved the quality of those horses that grazed in the plain below.

This year it was a great grey that carried Charles out to the road that clung to the face of the cliff. Behind him on a donkey, reminder of the humble beast that had borne

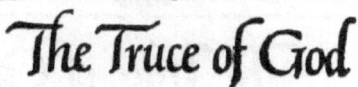

The Truce of God

the Christ into Jerusalem, rode the
Bishop. Saddled and bridled was
the grey, with a fierce head and
great shoulders, a strong beast for
strong days.

The men-at-arms were drawn up
in a double line, weapons at rest.
From the place below rose a thin
grey smoke where the fire kindled
for the steer. But the crowd had
deserted and now stood, eyes upraised to the Castle, and to the cliff
road where waited boys and men
ready for their desperate emprise,
clad in such protection of leather
as they could afford against the
stallion's hoofs.

Two people only remained by

29

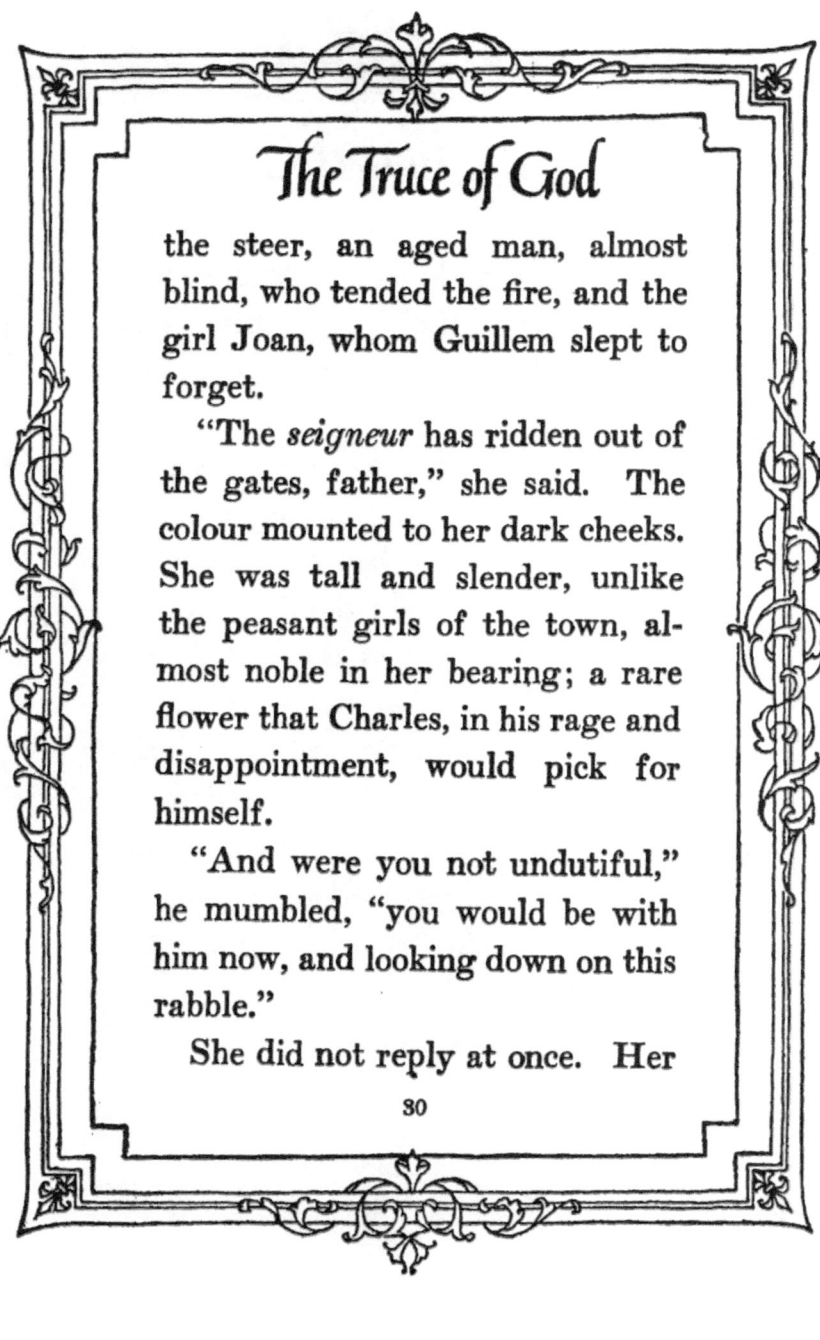

the steer, an aged man, almost blind, who tended the fire, and the girl Joan, whom Guillem slept to forget.

"The *seigneur* has ridden out of the gates, father," she said. The colour mounted to her dark cheeks. She was tall and slender, unlike the peasant girls of the town, almost noble in her bearing; a rare flower that Charles, in his rage and disappointment, would pick for himself.

"And were you not undutiful," he mumbled, "you would be with him now, and looking down on this rabble."

She did not reply at once. Her

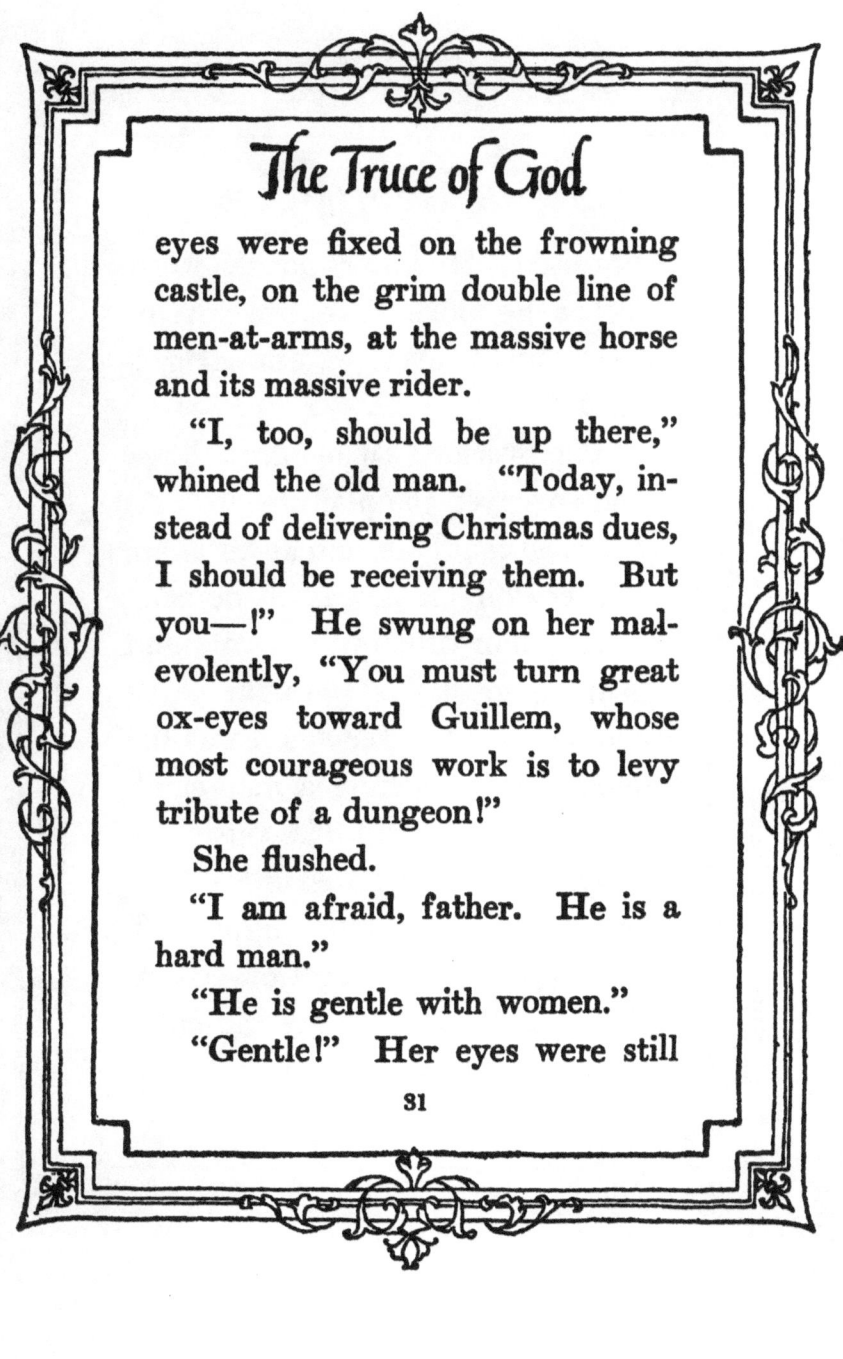

eyes were fixed on the frowning castle, on the grim double line of men-at-arms, at the massive horse and its massive rider.

"I, too, should be up there," whined the old man. "Today, instead of delivering Christmas dues, I should be receiving them. But you—!" He swung on her malevolently, "You must turn great ox-eyes toward Guillem, whose most courageous work is to levy tribute of a dungeon!"

She flushed.

"I am afraid, father. He is a hard man."

"He is gentle with women."

"Gentle!" Her eyes were still

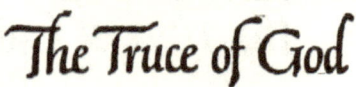

The Truce of God

upraised. "He knows not the word.
When he looks at me there is no
liking in his eyes. I am—frightened."

The overlord sat his great horse
and surveyed the plain below. As
far as he could see, and as far again
in every direction, was his domain,
paying him tithe of fat cattle and
heaping granaries. As far as he
could see and as far again was the
domain that, lacking a man-child,
would go to Philip, his cousin.

The Bishop, who rode his donkey without a saddle, slipped off
and stood beside the little beast on
the road. His finger absently
traced the dark cross on its back.

The Truce of God

"Idiots!" snarled the overlord out of his distemper, as he looked down into the faces of his faithful ones below. "Fools and sons of fools! Thy beast would suit them better, Bishop, than mine."

Then he flung himself insolently out of the saddle. There was little of Christmas in his heart, God knows; only hate and disappointment and thwarted pride.

"A great day, my lord," said the Bishop. "Peace over the land. The end of a plentiful year——"

"Bah!"

"The end of a plentiful year," repeated the Bishop tranquilly, "this day of His birth, a day for

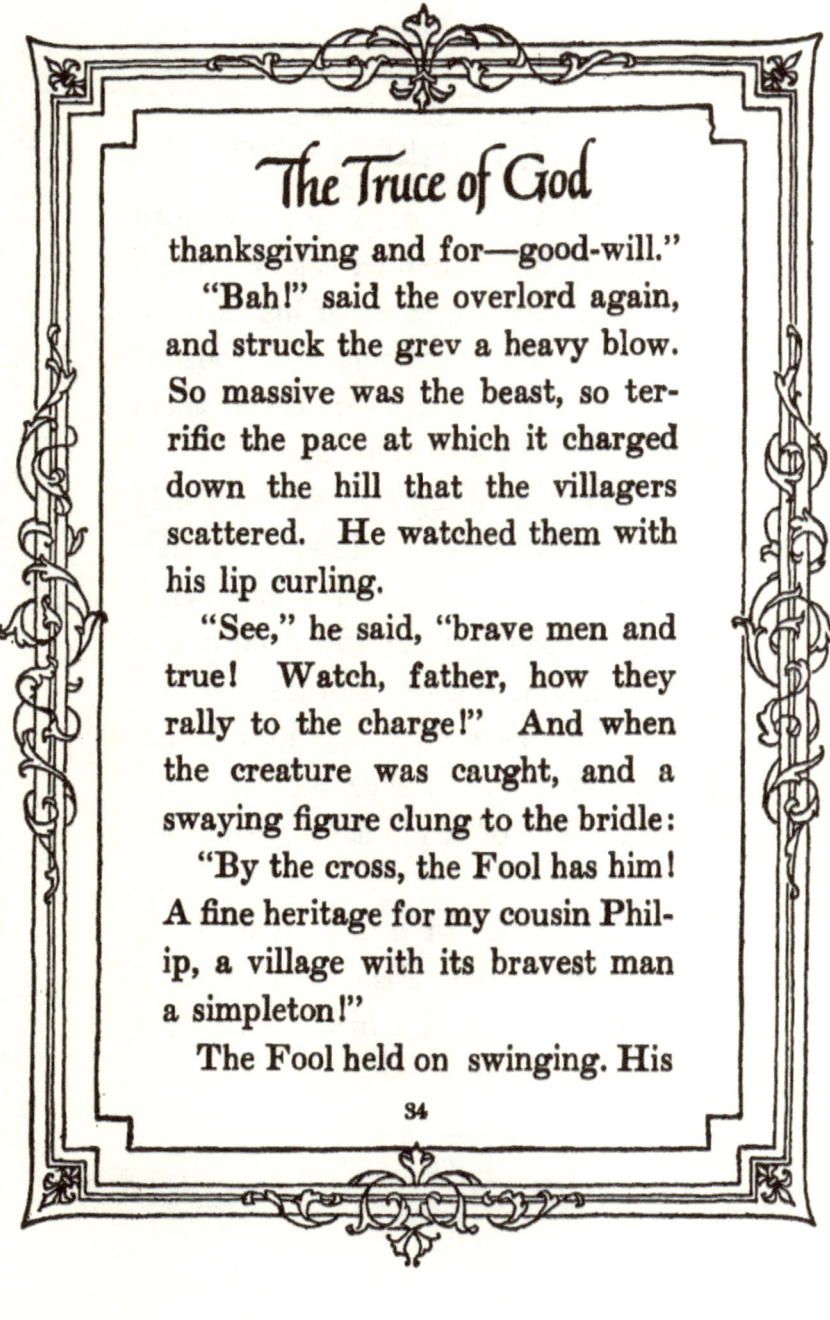

thanksgiving and for—good-will."

"Bah!" said the overlord again, and struck the grey a heavy blow. So massive was the beast, so terrific the pace at which it charged down the hill that the villagers scattered. He watched them with his lip curling.

"See," he said, "brave men and true! Watch, father, how they rally to the charge!" And when the creature was caught, and a swaying figure clung to the bridle:

"By the cross, the Fool has him! A fine heritage for my cousin Philip, a village with its bravest man a simpleton!"

The Fool held on swinging. His

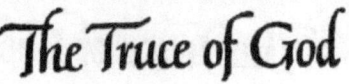

The Truce of God

arms were very strong, and as is
the way with fools and those that
drown, many things went through
his mind. The horse was his. He
would go adventuring along the
winter roads, adventuring and
singing. The townspeople gathered about him with sheepish
praise. From a dolt he had become
a hero. Many have taken the same
step in the same space of moments,
the line being but a line and easy to
cross.

The *dénouement* suited the grim
mood of the overlord. It pleased
him to see the smug villagers stand
by while the Fool mounted his
steed. Side by side from the para-

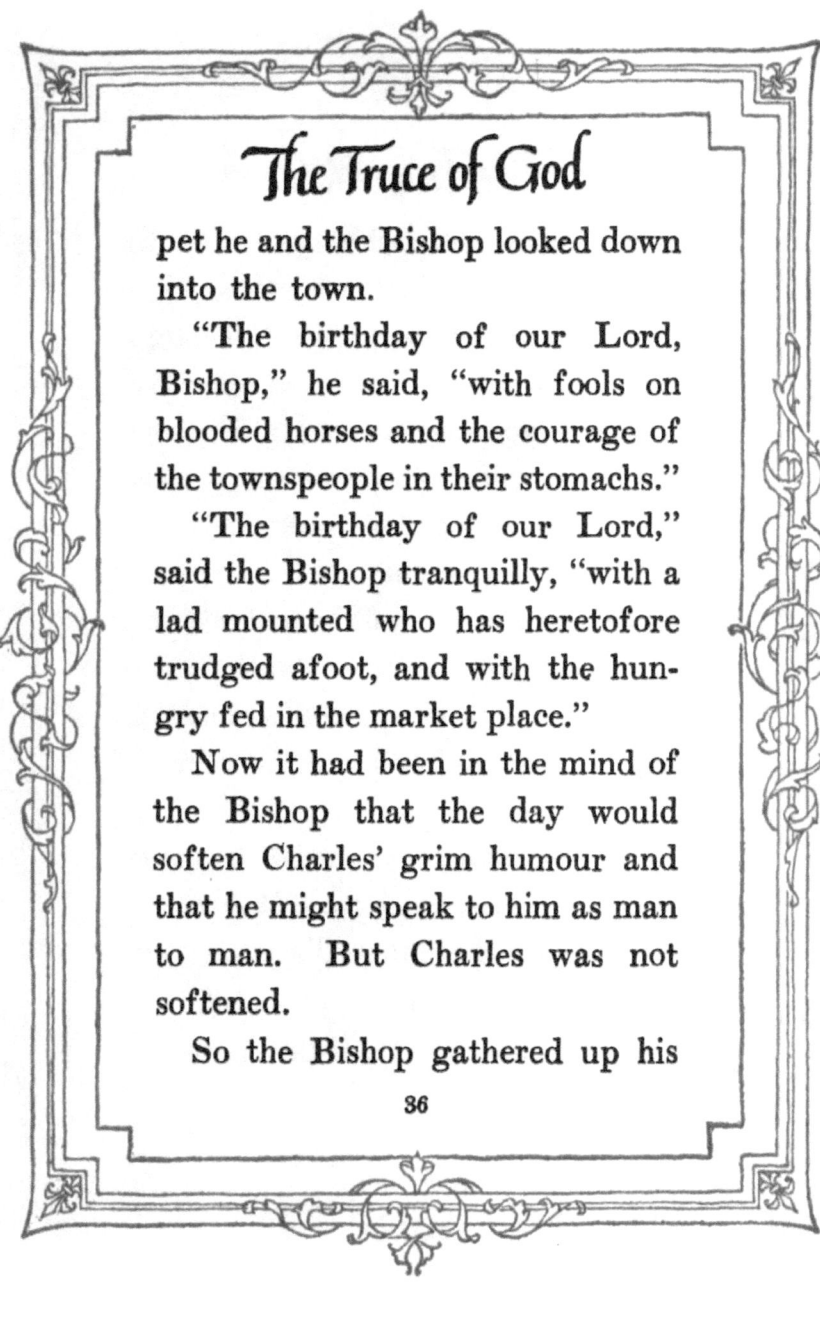

The Truce of God

pet he and the Bishop looked down into the town.

"The birthday of our Lord, Bishop," he said, "with fools on blooded horses and the courage of the townspeople in their stomachs."

"The birthday of our Lord," said the Bishop tranquilly, "with a lad mounted who has heretofore trudged afoot, and with the hungry fed in the market place."

Now it had been in the mind of the Bishop that the day would soften Charles' grim humour and that he might speak to him as man to man. But Charles was not softened.

So the Bishop gathered up his

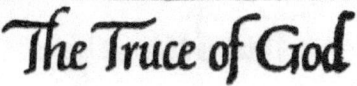

The Truce of God

courage. His hand was still on the cross on the donkey's back.

"You are young, my son, and have been grievously disappointed. I, who am old, have seen many things, and this I have learned. Two things there are that, next to the love of God, must be greatest in a man's life—not war nor slothful peace, nor pride, nor yet a will that would bend all things to its end."

The overlord scowled. He had found the girl Joan in the Market Square, and his eyes were on her.

"One," said the Bishop, "is the love of a woman. The other is— a child."

The Truce of God

The donkey stood meekly, with hanging head.

"A woman," repeated the Bishop. "You grow rough up here on your hillside. Only a few months since the lady your wife went away, and already order has forsaken you. The child, your daughter, runs like a wild thing, without control. Our Holy Church deplores these things."

"Will Holy Church grant me another wife?"

"Holy Church," replied the Bishop gravely, "would have you take back, my lord, the wife whom your hardness drove away."

The *seigneur's* gaze turned to

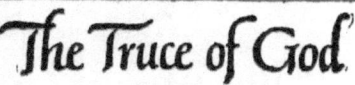

The Truce of God

the east, where lay the Castle of Philip, his cousin. Then he dropped brooding eyes to the Square below, where the girl Joan assisted her father by the fire, and moved like a mother of kings.

"You wish a woman for the castle, father," he said. "Then a woman we shall have. Holy Church may not give me another wife, but I shall take one. And I shall have a son."

. . . .

The child Clotilde had watched it all from a window. Because she was very high the thing she saw most plainly was the cross on the donkey's back. Far out over

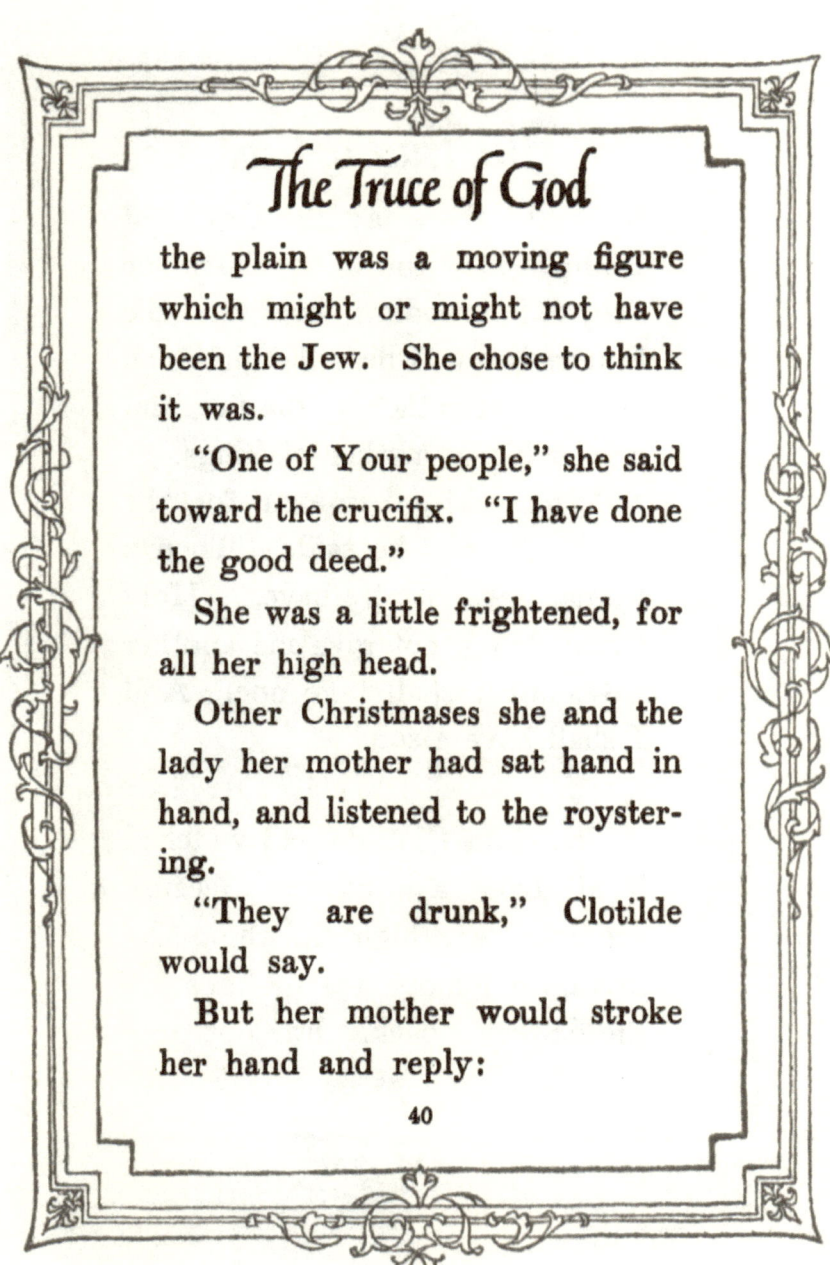

the plain was a moving figure which might or might not have been the Jew. She chose to think it was.

"One of Your people," she said toward the crucifix. "I have done the good deed."

She was a little frightened, for all her high head.

Other Christmases she and the lady her mother had sat hand in hand, and listened to the roystering.

"They are drunk," Clotilde would say.

But her mother would stroke her hand and reply:

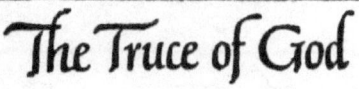

The Truce of God

"They but rejoice that our Lord is born."

So the child Clotilde stood at her window and gazed to where the plain stretched as far as she could see and as far again. And there was her mother. She would go to her and bring her back, or perhaps failing that, she might be allowed to stay.

Here no one would miss her. The odour of cooking food filled the great house, loud laughter, the clatter of mug on board. Her old nurse was below, decorating a boar's head with berries and a crown.

Because it was the Truce of

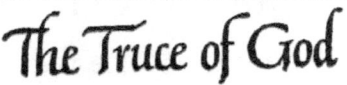

The Truce of God

God and a festival, the gates stood open. She reached the foot of the hill safely. Stragglers going up and down the steep way regarded her without suspicion. So she went through the Square past the roasting steer, and by a twisting street into the open country.

When she stopped to rest it was to look back with wistful eyes toward the frowning castle on the cliff. For a divided allegiance was hers. Passionately as she loved her mother, her indomitable spirit was her father's heritage, his fierceness was her courage, and she loved him as the small may love the great.

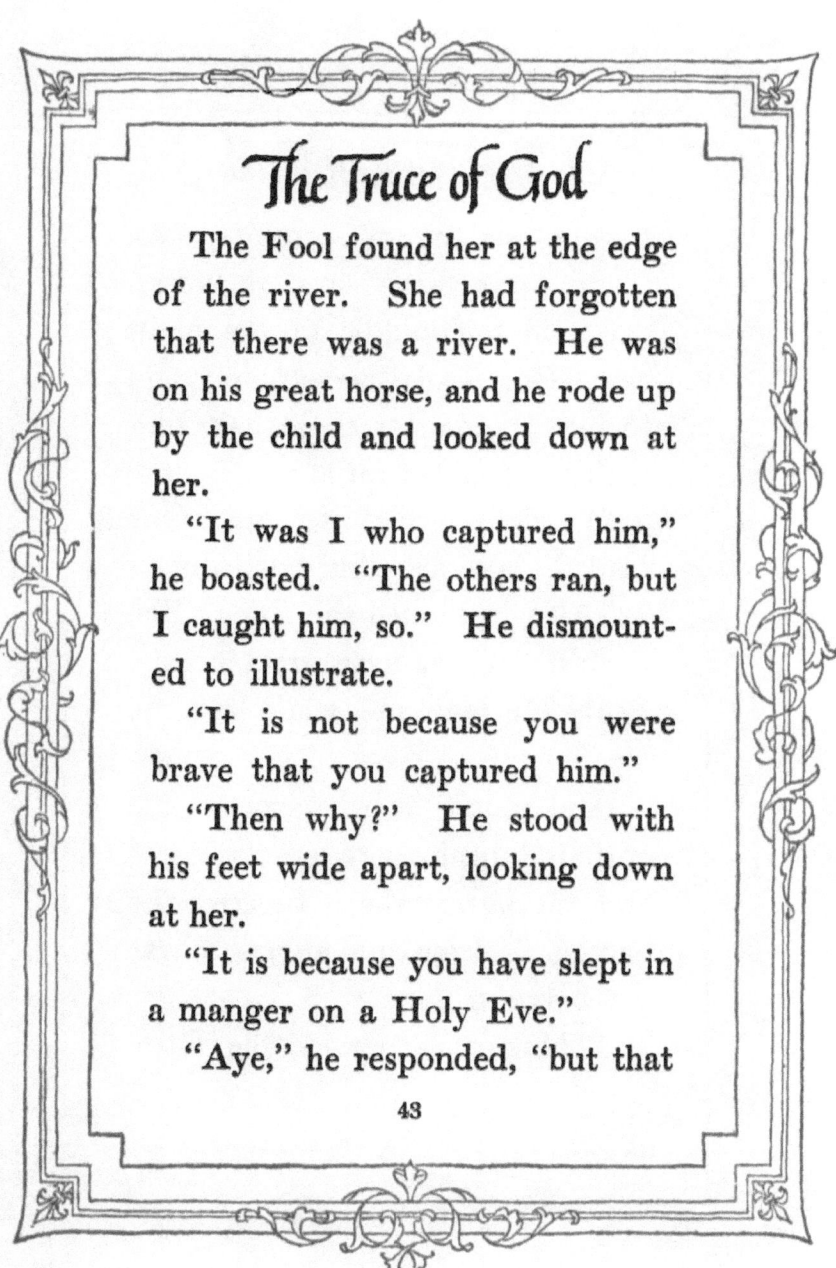

The Truce of God

The Fool found her at the edge of the river. She had forgotten that there was a river. He was on his great horse, and he rode up by the child and looked down at her.

"It was I who captured him," he boasted. "The others ran, but I caught him, so." He dismounted to illustrate.

"It is not because you were brave that you captured him."

"Then why?" He stood with his feet wide apart, looking down at her.

"It is because you have slept in a manger on a Holy Eve."

"Aye," he responded, "but that

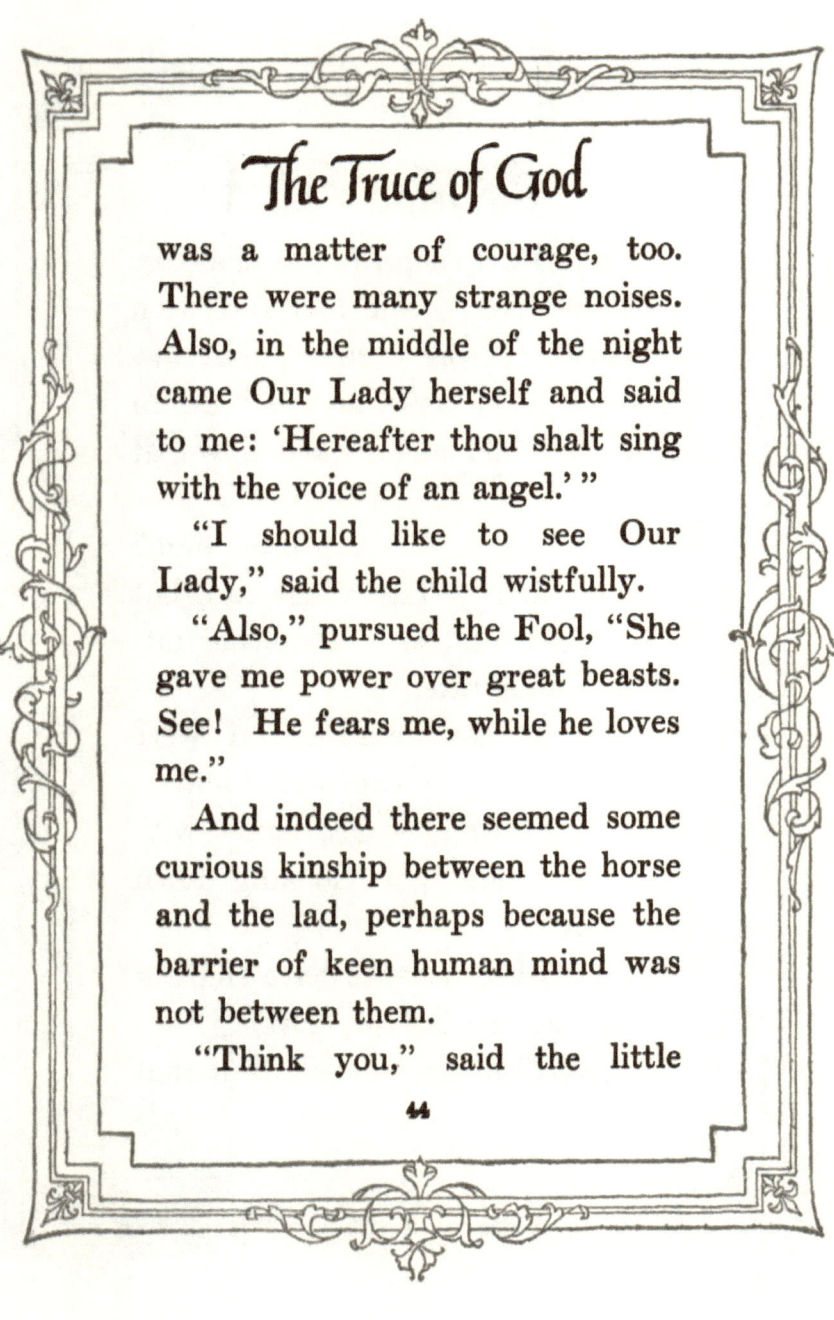

The Truce of God

was a matter of courage, too. There were many strange noises. Also, in the middle of the night came Our Lady herself and said to me: 'Hereafter thou shalt sing with the voice of an angel.'"

"I should like to see Our Lady," said the child wistfully.

"Also," pursued the Fool, "She gave me power over great beasts. See! He fears me, while he loves me."

And indeed there seemed some curious kinship between the horse and the lad, perhaps because the barrier of keen human mind was not between them.

"Think you," said the little

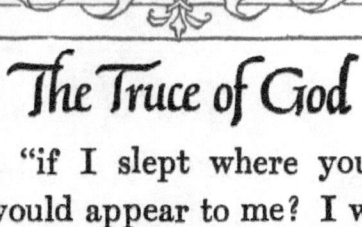

The Truce of God

maid, "if I slept where you did She would appear to me? I would not ask much, only to be made a lad like you, and, perhaps, to sing."

"But I am a simpleton. Instead of wit I have but a voice and now—a horse."

"A lad like you," she persisted, "so that my father would love me and my mother might come back again?"

"Better stay as you are," said the Fool. "Also, there will be no Holy Eve again for a long time. It comes but once a year. Also it is hard times for men who must either fight or work in the fields. I——" He struck his chest. "I shall do neither. And I shall cut no more wood. I go adventuring."

Clotilde rose and drew her grey cloak around her.

"I am adventuring, too," she said. "Only I have no voice and no horse. May I go with you?"

The boy was doubtful. He had that innate love and tenderness that is given to his kind instead of other things. But a child!

"I will take you," he said at last, rather heavily. "But where, little lady?"

"To my mother at the castle of Black Philip." And when his

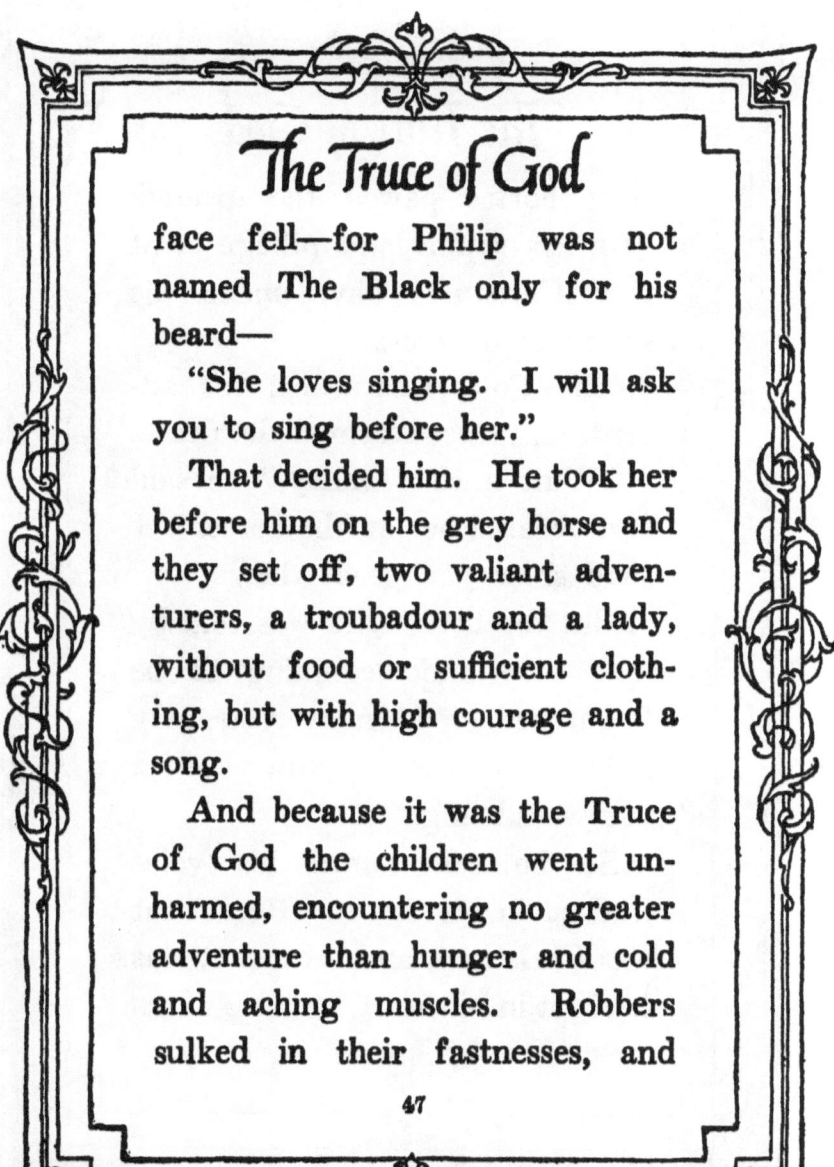

face fell—for Philip was not named The Black only for his beard—

"She loves singing. I will ask you to sing before her."

That decided him. He took her before him on the grey horse and they set off, two valiant adventurers, a troubadour and a lady, without food or sufficient clothing, but with high courage and a song.

And because it was the Truce of God the children went unharmed, encountering no greater adventure than hunger and cold and aching muscles. Robbers sulked in their fastnesses, and

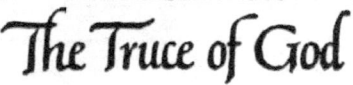

The Truce of God

their horses pawed the ground. Murder, rapine and pillage slept that Christmas day, under the shelter of the cross.

The Fool, who ached for adventure, rather resented the peace.

"Wait until Monday," he said from behind her on the horse. "I shall show you great things."

But the little maid was cold by that time and beginning to be frightened. "Monday you may fight," she said. "Now I wish you would sing."

So he sang until his voice cracked in his throat. Because it was Christmas, and because it was freshest in his heart, he sang most-

48

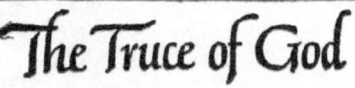

The Truce of God

ly what he and the blacksmith and the crockery-seller had sung in the castle yard:

"The Light of Light Divine,
True Brightness undefiled,
He bears for us the shame of sin,
A holy, spotless Child."

They lay that night in a ruined barn with a roof of earth and stones. Clotilde eyed the manger wistfully, but the Holy Eve was past, and the day of miracles would not come for a year.

Toward morning, however, she roused the boy with a touch.

"She may have forgotten me," she said. "She has been gone since the spring. She may not love me now."

49

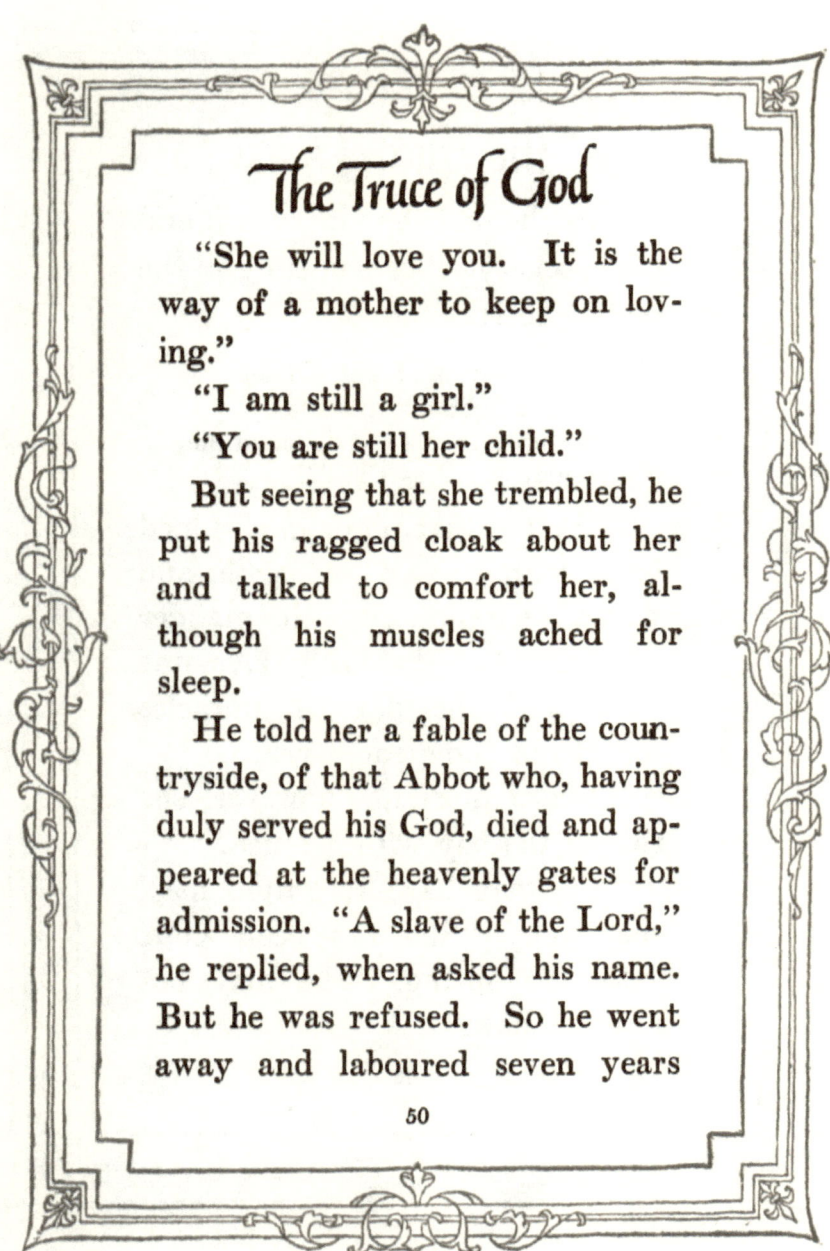

"She will love you. It is the way of a mother to keep on loving."

"I am still a girl."

"You are still her child."

But seeing that she trembled, he put his ragged cloak about her and talked to comfort her, although his muscles ached for sleep.

He told her a fable of the countryside, of that Abbot who, having duly served his God, died and appeared at the heavenly gates for admission. "A slave of the Lord," he replied, when asked his name. But he was refused. So he went away and laboured seven years again at good deeds and returned. "A servant of the Lord," he called himself, and again he was refused. Yet another seven years he laboured and came in all humility to the gate. "A child of the Lord," said the Abbot, who had gained both wisdom and humility. And the gates opened.

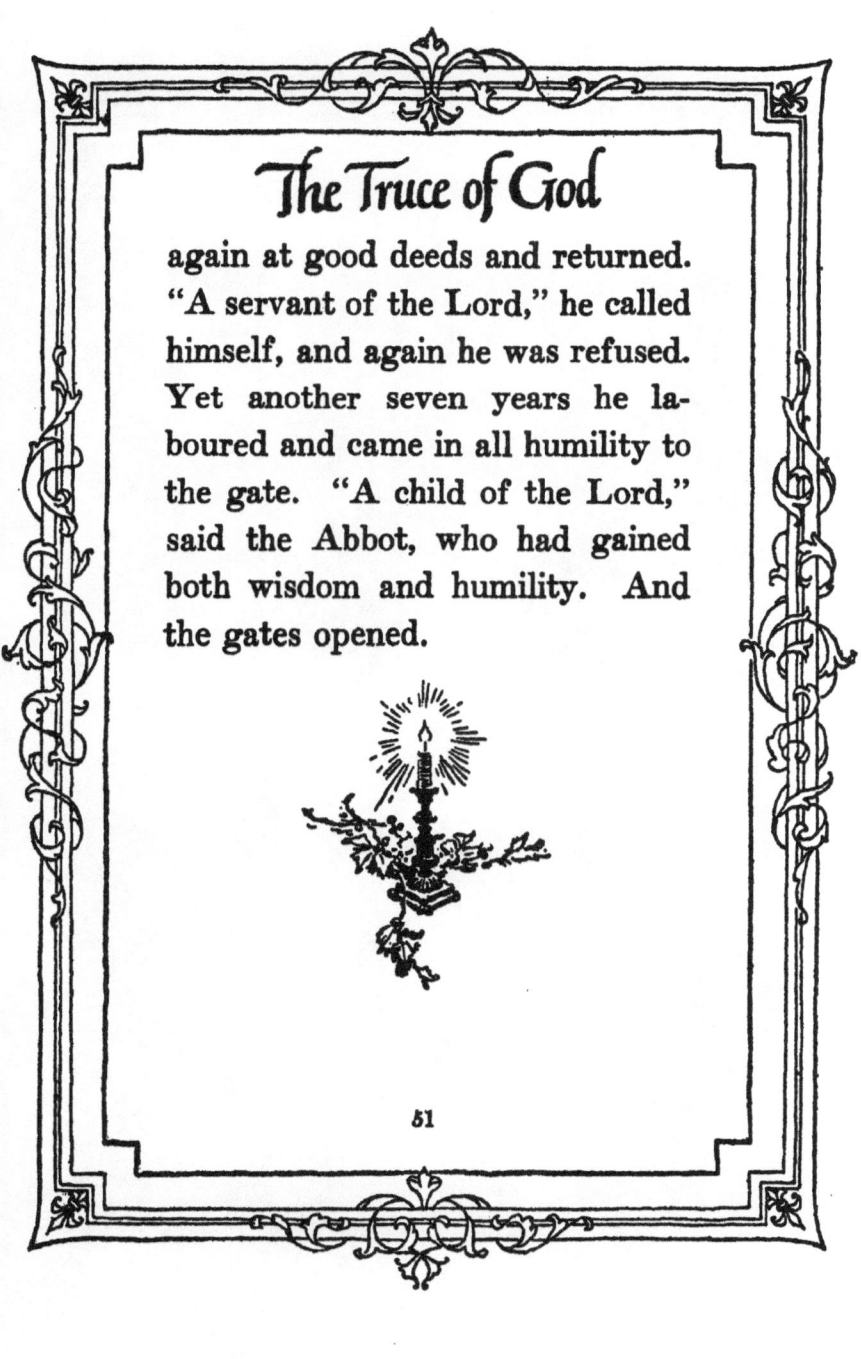

Chapter
Three

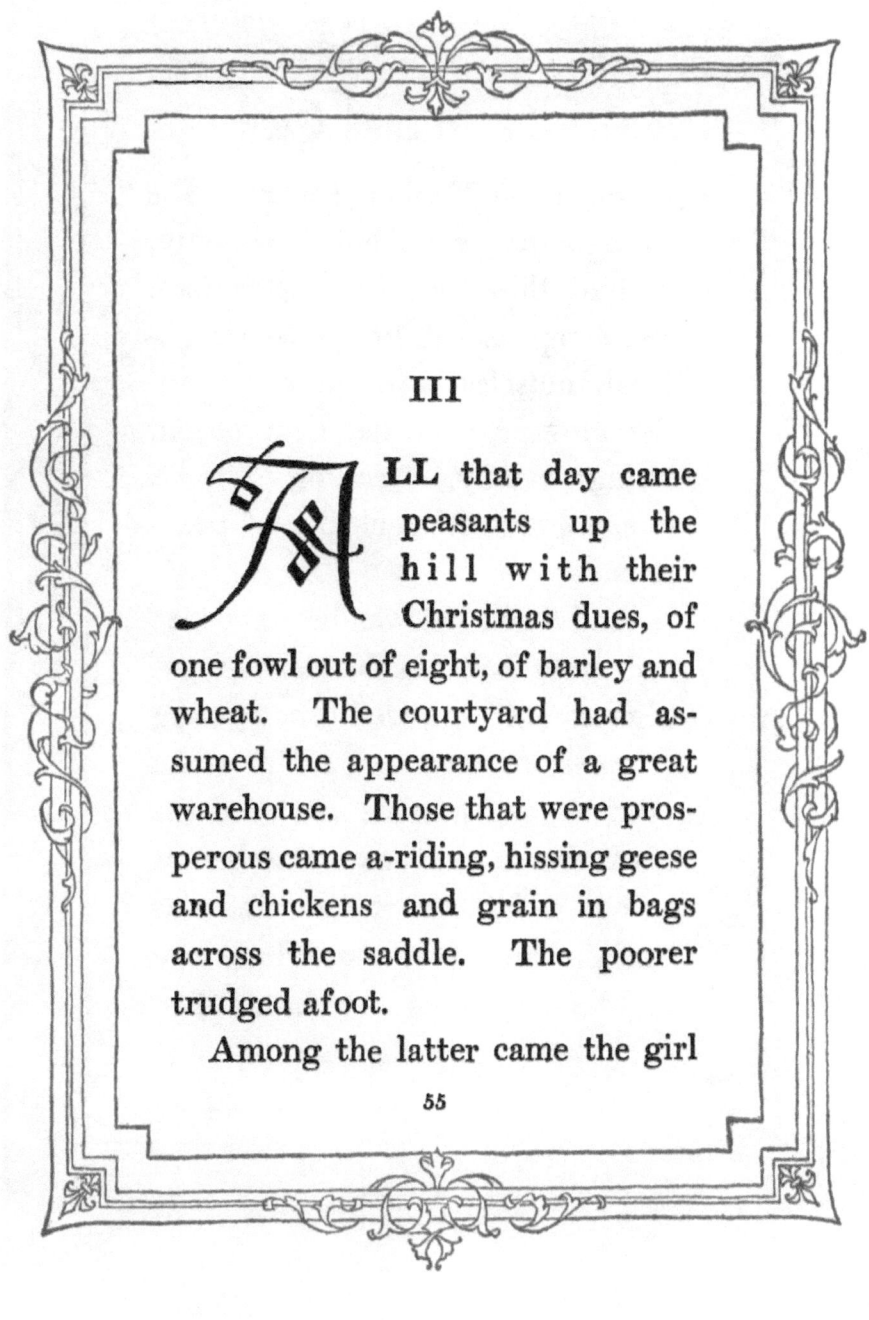

III

ALL that day came peasants up the hill with their Christmas dues, of one fowl out of eight, of barley and wheat. The courtyard had assumed the appearance of a great warehouse. Those that were prosperous came a-riding, hissing geese and chickens and grain in bags across the saddle. The poorer trudged afoot.

Among the latter came the girl

The Truce of God

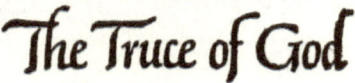

Joan of the Market Square. She brought no grain, but fowls only, and of these but two. She took the steep ascent like a thorough-bred, muscles working clean under glowing skin, her deep bosom rising evenly, treading like a queen among that clutter of peasants.

And when she was brought into the great hall her head went yet higher. It pleased the young *seigneur* to be gracious. But he eyed her much as he had eyed the great horse that morning before he cut it with the whip. She was but a means to an end. Such love and tenderness as were in him had

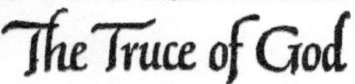
The Truce of God

gone out to the gentle wife he had put away from him, and had died—of Clotilde.

So Charles appraised her and found her, although but a means, very beautiful. Only the Bishop turned away his head.

"Joan," said Charles, "do you know why I have sent for you?"

The girl looked down. But, although she quivered, it was not with fright.

"I do, sire."

Something of a sardonic smile played around the *seigneur's* mouth. The butterfly came too quietly to the net.

"We are but gloomy folk here,

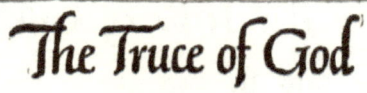

The Truce of God

rough soldiers and few women.
It has been in my mind——" Here
he saw the Bishop's averted head,
and scowled. What had been in
his mind he forgot. He said: "I
would have you come willingly,
or not at all."

At that she lifted her head and
looked at him. "You know I will
come," she said. "I can do nothing else, but I do not come willingly, my lord. You are asking
too much."

The Bishop turned his head
hopefully.

"Why?"

"You are a hard man, my lord."

If she meant to anger him, she

failed. They were not soft days. A man hid such tenderness as he had under grimness, and prayed in the churches for phlegm.

"I am a fighting man. I have no gentle ways." Then a belated memory came to him. "I give no tenderness and ask none. But such kindness as you have, lavish on the child Clotilde. She is much alone."

With the mention of Clotilde's name came a vision: instead of this splendid peasant wench he seemed to see the graceful and drooping figure of the woman he had put away because she had not borne him a son. He closed his

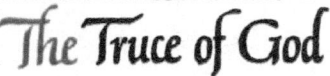

eyes, and the girl, taking it for dismissal, went away.

When he opened them there were only the fire and the dogs about it, and the Bishop, who was preparing to depart.

"I shall not stay, my lord," said the Bishop. "The thing is desecration. No good can come from such a bond. It is Christmas and the Truce of God, and yet you do this evil thing."

So the Bishop went, muffled in a cloak, and mantled with displeasure. And with him, now that Clotilde had fled, went all that was good and open to the sun,

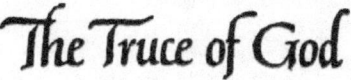

The Truce of God

from the grey castle of Charles the Fair.

At evening Joan came again, still afoot, but now clad in her best. She came alone, and the men at the gates, instructed, let her in. She gazed around the courtyard with its burden of grain that had been crushed out of her people below, with its loitering soldiers and cackling fowls, and she shivered as the gates closed behind her.

She was a good girl, as the times went, and she knew well that she had been brought up the hill as the stallion that morning had been driven down. She remem-

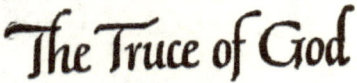

The Truce of God

bered the cut of the whip, and in the twilight of the courtyard she stretched out her arms toward the little town below, where the old man, her father, lived in semi-darkness, and where on that Christmas evening the women were gathered in the churches to pray.

Having no seasonable merriment in himself, Charles surrounded himself that night with cheer. A band of wandering minstrels had arrived to sing, the great fire blazed, the dogs around it gnawed the bones of the Christmas feast. But when the troubadours would have sung of the Nativity, he bade

The Truce of God

them in a great voice to have done. So they sang of war, and, remembering his cousin Philip, his eyes blazed.

When Joan came he motioned her to a seat beside him, not on his right, but on his left, and there he let her sit without speech. But his mind was working busily. He would have a son and the King would legitimise him. Then let Philip go hang. These lands of his as far as the eye could reach and as far again would never go to him.

The minstrels sang of war, and of his own great deeds, but there was no one of them with so beau-

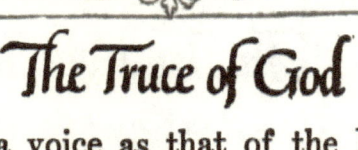

The Truce of God

tiful a voice as that of the Fool, who could sing only of peace. And the Fool was missing.

However, their songs soothed his hurt pride. This was he; these things he had done. If the Bishop had not turned sour and gone, he would have heard what they sang. He might have understood, too, the craving of a man's warrior soul for a warrior son, for one to hold what he had gathered at such cost. Back always to this burning hope of his!

Joan sat on his left hand, and went hot and cold, hot with shame and cold with fear.

So now, his own glory as a war-

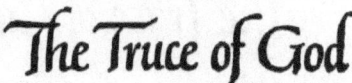
The Truce of God

rior commencing to pall on him,
Charles would have more tribute,
this time as lord of peace. He
would celebrate this day of days,
and at the same time throw a sop
to Providence.

He would release the Jew.

The troubadours sang louder;
fresh liquor was passed about.
Charles waited for the Jew to be
brought.

He remembered Clotilde then.
She should see him do this noble
thing. Since her mother had gone
she had shrunk from him. Now
let her see how magnanimous he
could be. He, the *seigneur*, who
held life and death in his hands,

The Truce of God

would this day give, not death, but life.

Being not displeased with himself, he turned at last toward Joan and put a hand over hers.

"You see," he said, "I am not so hard a man. By this Christian act shall I celebrate your arrival."

But the Jew did not come. The singers learned the truth, and sang with watchful eyes. The *seigneur's* anger was known to be mighty, and to strike close at hand.

Guillem, the gaoler, had been waiting for the summons.

News had come to him late in the afternoon that had made him indifferent to his fate. The girl

The Truce of God

Joan, whom he loved, had come up the hill at the overlord's summons. So, instead of raising an alarm, Guillem had waited sullenly. Death, which yesterday he would have blenched to behold, now beckoned him. When he was brought in, he stood with folded arms and asked no mercy.

"He is gone, my lord," said Guillem, and waited. He did not glance at the girl.

"Gone?" said Charles. Then he laughed, such laughter as turned the girl cold.

"Gone, earth-clod? How now? Perhaps you, too, wished to give

67

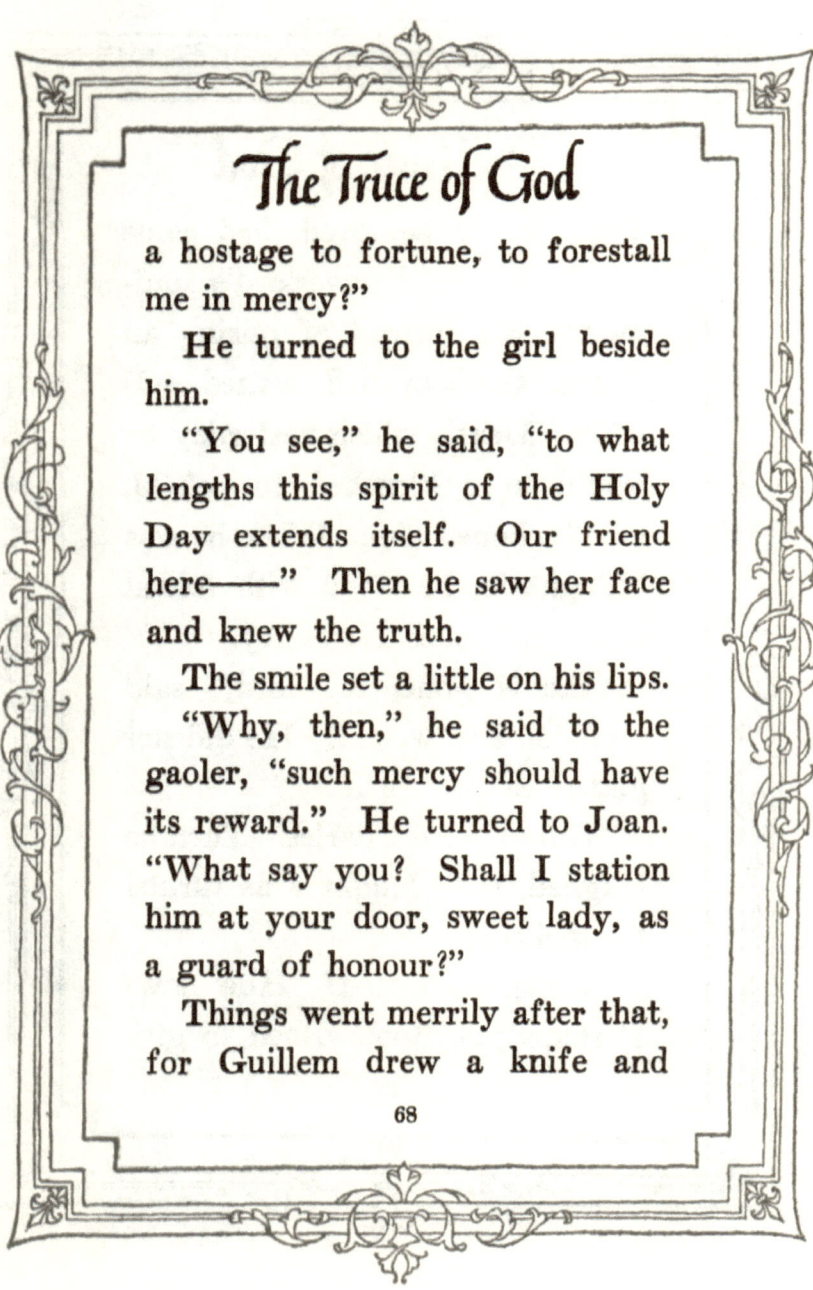

a hostage to fortune, to forestall me in mercy?"

He turned to the girl beside him.

"You see," he said, "to what lengths this spirit of the Holy Day extends itself. Our friend here——" Then he saw her face and knew the truth.

The smile set a little on his lips.

"Why, then," he said to the gaoler, "such mercy should have its reward." He turned to Joan. "What say you? Shall I station him at your door, sweet lady, as a guard of honour?"

Things went merrily after that, for Guillem drew a knife and

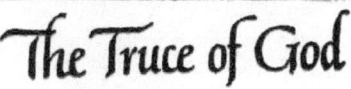

The Truce of God

made, not for the *seigneur,* but for Joan. The troubadours feared to stop singing without a signal, so they sang through white lips. The dogs gnawed at their bones and the *seigneur* sat and smiled, showing his teeth.

Guillem, finally unhanded, stood with folded arms and waited for death.

"It is the time of the Truce of God," said the *seigneur* softly, and, knowing that death would be a boon, sent him off unhurt.

The village, which had eaten full, slept early that night. Down the hill at nine o'clock came half a

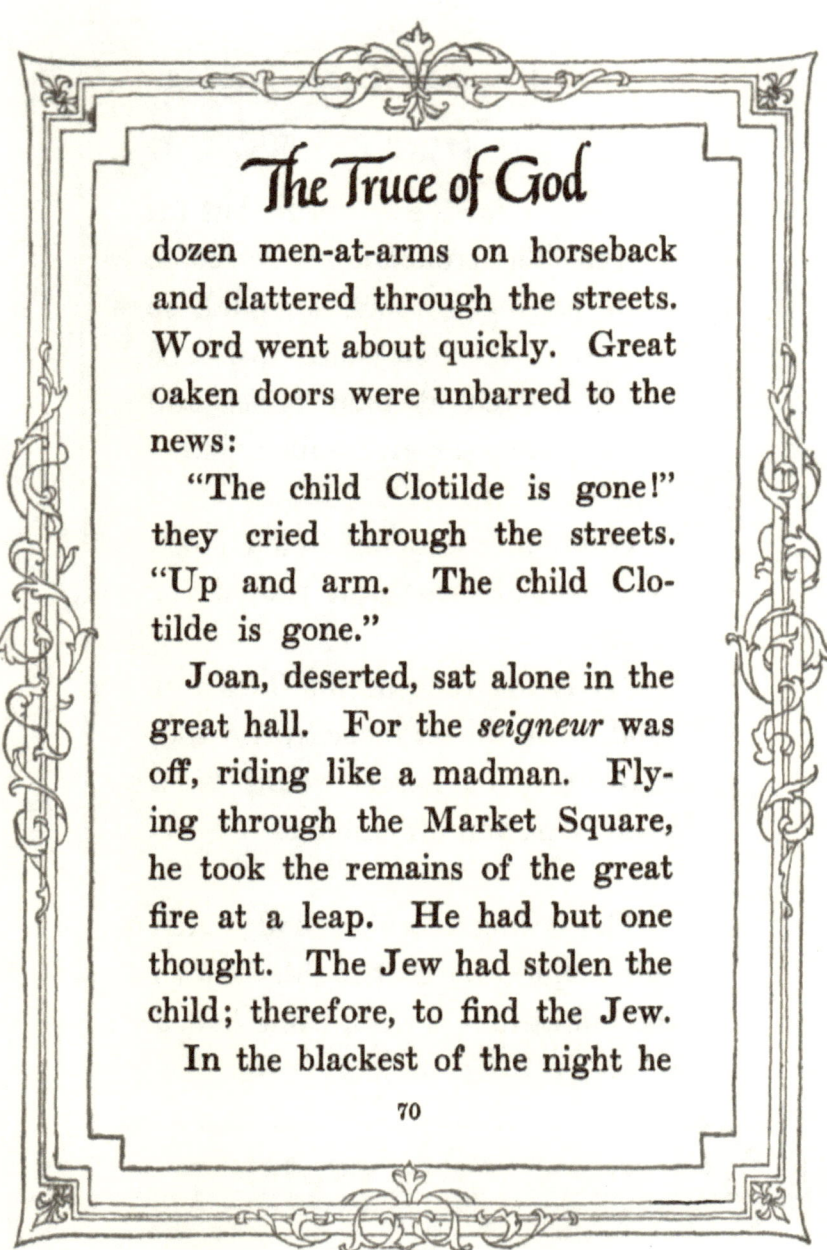

The Truce of God

dozen men-at-arms on horseback and clattered through the streets. Word went about quickly. Great oaken doors were unbarred to the news:

"The child Clotilde is gone!" they cried through the streets. "Up and arm. The child Clotilde is gone."

Joan, deserted, sat alone in the great hall. For the *seigneur* was off, riding like a madman. Flying through the Market Square, he took the remains of the great fire at a leap. He had but one thought. The Jew had stolen the child; therefore, to find the Jew.

In the blackest of the night he

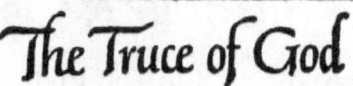

The Truce of God

found him, sitting by the road, bent over his staff. The eyes he raised to Charles were haggard and weary. Charles reined his horse back on his haunches, his men-at-arms behind him.

"What have you done with the child?"

"The child?"

"Out with it," cried Charles and flung himself from his horse. If the Jew were haggard, Charles was more so, hard bitten of terror, pallid to the lips.

"I have seen no child. That is——" He hastened to correct himself, seeing Charles' face in the light of a torch. "I was released by a child, a girl. I have not seen her since."

He spoke with the simplicity of truth. In the light of the torches Charles' face went white.

"She released you?" he repeated slowly. "What did she say?"

"She said: 'It is the birthday of our Lord,'" repeated the Jew, slowly, out of his weary brain. "'And I am doing a good deed.'"

"Is that all?" The Jew hesitated.

"Also she said: 'But you do not love our Lord.'"

Charles swore under his breath. "And you?"

"I said but little. I——"

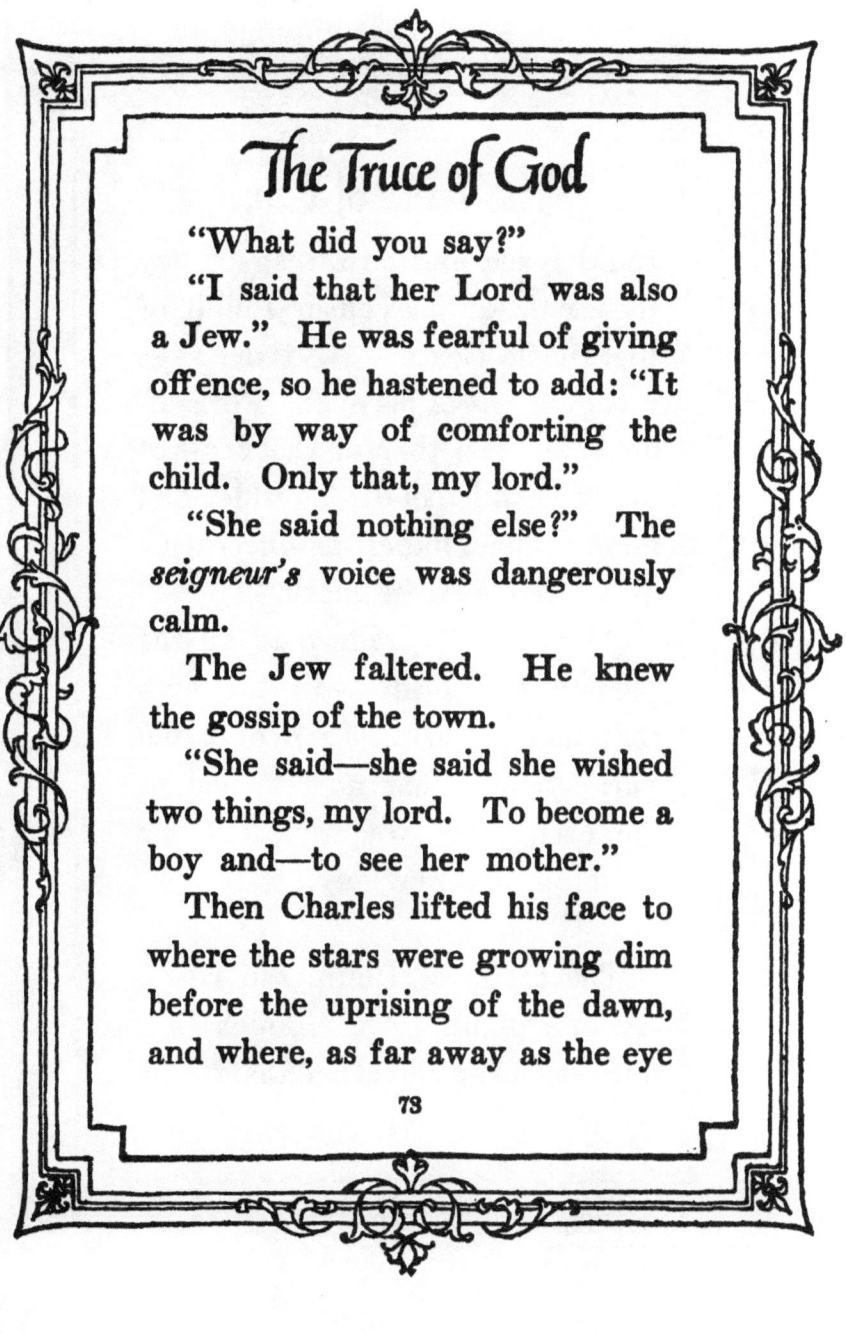

The Truce of God

"What did you say?"

"I said that her Lord was also a Jew." He was fearful of giving offence, so he hastened to add: "It was by way of comforting the child. Only that, my lord."

"She said nothing else?" The *seigneur's* voice was dangerously calm.

The Jew faltered. He knew the gossip of the town.

"She said—she said she wished two things, my lord. To become a boy and—to see her mother."

Then Charles lifted his face to where the stars were growing dim before the uprising of the dawn, and where, as far away as the eye

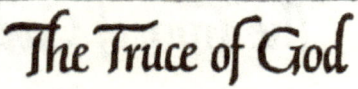

could reach and as far again, lay the castle of his cousin Philip of the Black Beard. And the rage was gone out of his eyes. For suddenly he knew that, on that feast of mother and child, Clotilde had gone to her mother, as unerringly as an arrow to its mark.

And with the rage died all the passion and pride. In the eyes that had gazed at Joan over the parapet, and that now turned to the east, there was reflected the dawning of a new day.

The castle of Philip the Black lay in a plain. For as much as a mile in every direction the forest

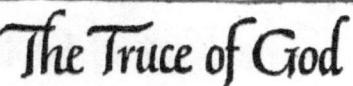

The Truce of God

had been sacrificed against the
loving advances of his cousin
Charles. Also about the castle
was a moat in which swam noisy
geese and much litter.

When, shortly after dawn, the
sentry at the drawbridge saw a
great horse with a double burden
crossing the open space he was
but faintly interested. A belated
peasant with his Christmas dues,
perhaps. But when, on the lift-
ing of the morning haze, he saw
that the horse bore two children
and one a girl, he called another
man to look.

"Troubadours, by the sound,"
said the newcomer. For the Fool

75

was singing to cheer his lack of breakfast. "Coming empty of belly, as come all troubadours."

But the sentry was dubious. Minstrels were a slothful lot, averse to the chill of early morning.

And when the pair came nearer and drew up beyond the moat, the soldiers were still at a loss. The Fool's wandering eyes and tender mouth bespoke him no troubadour, and the child rode with head high like a princess.

"I have come to see my mother," Clotilde called, and demanded admission, clearly.

Here were no warriors, but a

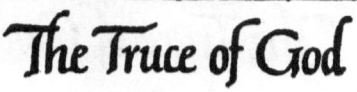

The Truce of God

Fool and a child. So they let down the bridge and admitted the pair. But they raised the bridge at once again against the loving advances of Philip's cousin Charles.

But once in the courtyard Clotilde's courage began to fail her. Would her mother want her? Prayer had been unavailing and she was still a girl. And, at first, it seemed as though her fears had been justified, although they took her into the castle kindly enough, and offered her food which she could not eat and plied her with questions which she could not answer.

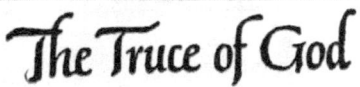

"I want my mother," was the only thing they could get out of her. Her little body was taut as a bowstring, her lips tight. They offered her excuses; the lady mother slept; now she was rising and must be clothed. And then at last they told her, because of the hunted look in her eyes.

"She is ill," they said. "Wait but a little and you shall see her."

Deadly despair had Clotilde in its grasp with that announcement. These strange folk were gentle enough with her, but never before had her mother refused her the haven of her out-held arms. Besides, they lied. Their eyes were

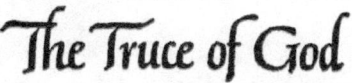

The Truce of God

shifty. She could see in their faces that they kept something from her.

Philip, having confessed himself overnight, by candle-light, was at mass when the pair arrived. Three days one must rot of peace, and those three days, to be not entirely lost, he prayed for success against Charles, or for another thing that lay close to his heart. But not for both together, since that was not possible.

He knelt stiffly in his cold chapel and made his supplications, but he was not too engrossed to hear the drawbridge chains and to pick up his ears to the clatter of the grey horse.

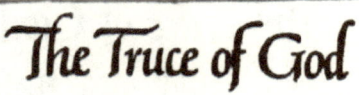

The Truce of God

So, having been communicated, he made short shift of what remained to be done, and got to his feet.

The Abbot, whose offices were finished, had also heard the drawbridge chains and let him go.

When Philip saw Clotilde he frowned and then smiled. He had sons, but no daughter, and he would have set her on his shoulder. But she drew away haughtily.

So Philip sat in a chair and watched her with a curious smile playing about his lips. Surely it were enough to make him smile, that he should play host to the wife

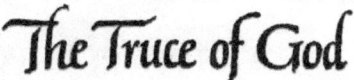

The Truce of God

and daughter of his cousin Charles.

Because of that, and of the thing that he had prayed for, and with a twinkle in his eyes, Black Philip alternately watched the child, and from a window the plain which was prepared against his cousin. And, as he had expected, at ten o'clock in the morning came Charles and six men-at-arms, riding like demons, and jerked up their horses at the edge of the moat.

Philip, still with the smile under his black beard, went out to greet them.

"Well met, cousin," he called; "you ride fast and early."

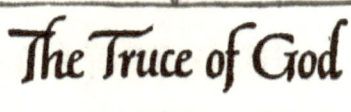

The Truce of God

Charles eyed him with feverish eyes.

"Truce of God," he said, sulkily, from across the moat. And then: "We seek a runaway, the child Clotilde."

"I shall make inquiry," said Philip, veiling the twinkle under his heavy brow. "In such a season many come and go."

But in his eyes Charles read the truth, and breathed with freer breath.

They lowered the drawbridge again with a great creaking of windlass and chain, and Charles with his head up rode across. But his men-at-arms stood their horses squarely on the bridge so that it could not be raised, and Philip smiled into his beard.

Charles dismounted stiffly. He had been a night in the saddle and his horse staggered with fatigue. In Philip's courtyard, as in his own, were piled high the Christmas tithes.

"A good year," said Philip agreeably, and indicated the dues. "Peaceful times, eh, cousin?"

But Charles only turned to see that his men kept the drawbridge open, and followed him into the house. Once inside, however, he turned on Philip fiercely.

"I am not here of my own de-

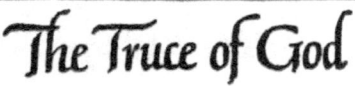

sire. It appears that both my wife and child find sanctuary with you."

"Tut," said Philip, good-naturedly, "it is the Christmas season, man, and a Sunday. We will not quarrel as to the why of your coming."

"Where is she?"

"Your wife or Clotilde?"

Now all through the early morning Charles had longed for one as for the other. But there was nothing of that in his voice.

"Clotilde," he said.

"I shall make inquiry if she has arrived," mumbled Philip into his beard, and went away.

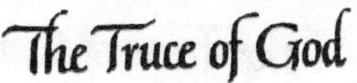

The Truce of God

So it came about that Charles was alone when he saw the child and caught her up in his hungry arms. As for Clotilde, her fear died at once in his embrace. When Philip returned he found them thus and coughed discreetly. So Charles released the child and put her on her feet.

"I have," said Philip, "another member of your family under my roof as to whom you have made no inquiry."

"I have secured that for which I came," said Charles haughtily.

But his eyes were on Philip and a question was in them. Philip, however, was not minded to play

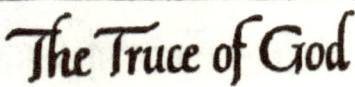

The Truce of God

Charles' game, but his own, and that not too fast.

"In that event, cousin," he replied, "let the little maid eat and then take her away. And since it is a Sunday and the Truce of God, we can drink to the Christmas season. Even quarrelling dogs have intervals of peace."

So perforce, because the question was still in his heart if not in his eyes, Charles drank with his cousin and enemy Philip. But with his hand in that small hand of Clotilde's which was so like her mother's.

Philip's expansiveness extended itself to the men-at-arms who still

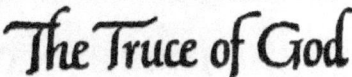

The Truce of God

sat woodenly on the drawbridge. He sent them hot liquor, for the day was cold, and at such intervals as Charles' questioning eyes were turned away, he rubbed his hands together furtively, as a man with a secret.

"A prosperous year," said Philip.

Charles grunted.

"We shall have snow before night," said Philip.

"Humph!" said Charles and glanced toward the sky, but made no move to go.

"The child is growing."

To this Charles made no reply whatever and Philip bleated on.

The Truce of God

"Her mother's body," he said, "but your eyes and hair, cousin."

Charles could stand no more. He pushed the child away and rose to his feet. Philip, to give him no tithe of advantage, rose too.

"Now," said Charles squarely, "where is my wife? Is she hiding from me?"

Then Philip's face must grow very grave and his mouth set in sad lines.

"She is ill, Charles. I would have told you sooner, but you lacked interest."

Charles swallowed to steady his voice.

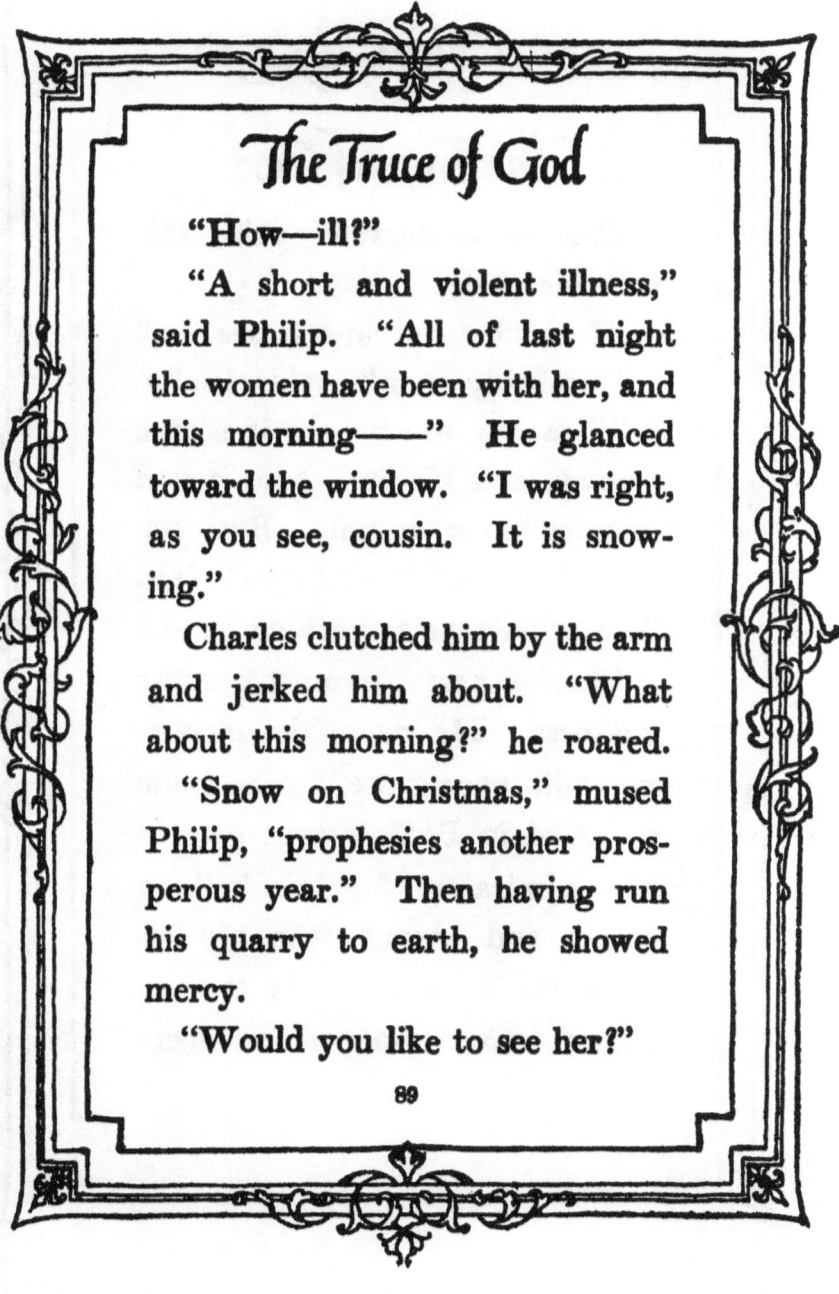

The Truce of God

"How—ill?"

"A short and violent illness," said Philip. "All of last night the women have been with her, and this morning——" He glanced toward the window. "I was right, as you see, cousin. It is snowing."

Charles clutched him by the arm and jerked him about. "What about this morning?" he roared.

"Snow on Christmas," mused Philip, "prophesies another prosperous year." Then having run his quarry to earth, he showed mercy.

"Would you like to see her?"

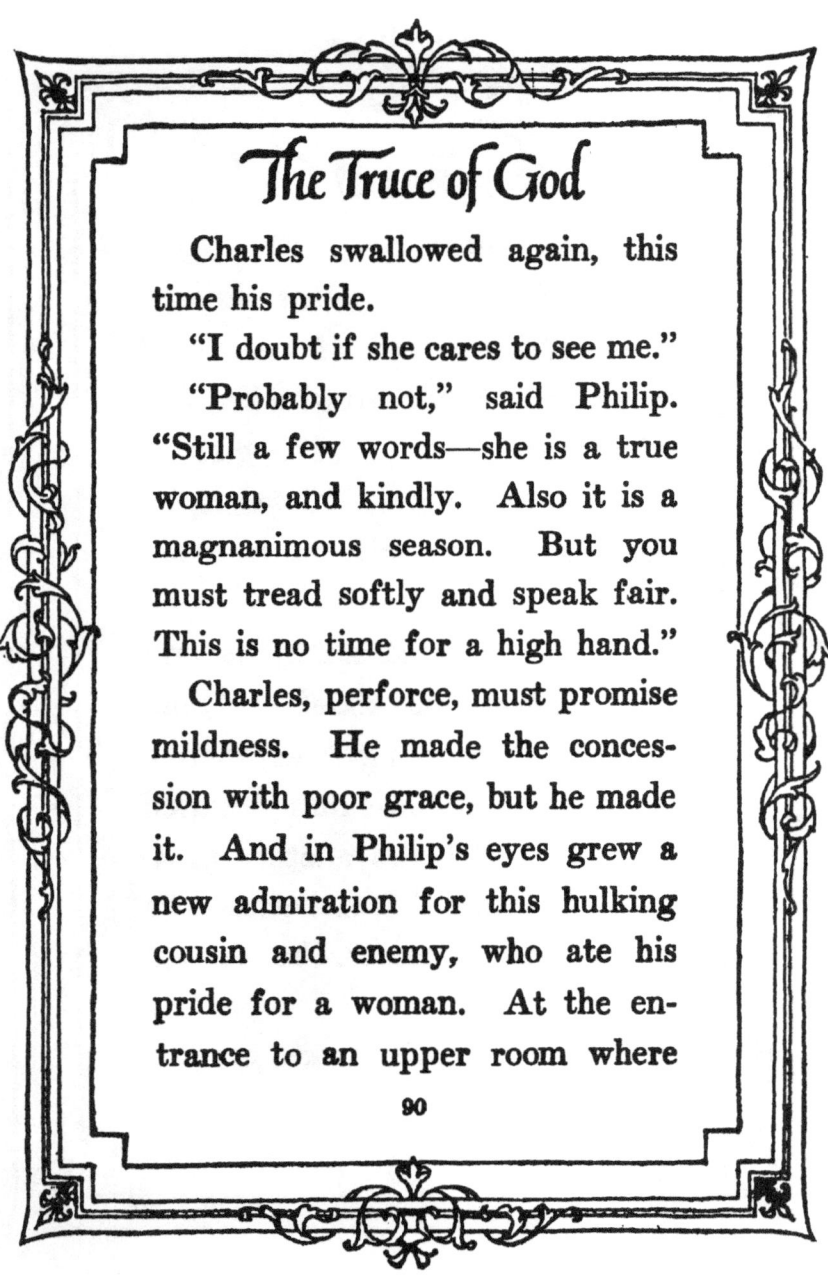

The Truce of God

Charles swallowed again, this time his pride.

"I doubt if she cares to see me."

"Probably not," said Philip. "Still a few words—she is a true woman, and kindly. Also it is a magnanimous season. But you must tread softly and speak fair. This is no time for a high hand."

Charles, perforce, must promise mildness. He made the concession with poor grace, but he made it. And in Philip's eyes grew a new admiration for this hulking cousin and enemy, who ate his pride for a woman. At the entrance to an upper room where hung a leather curtain, he stood aside.

"Softly," he said through his beard. "No harsh words. Send the child in first."

So Philip went ponderously away and left Charles to cool his heels and wait. As he stood there sheepishly he remembered many things with shame. Joan, and the violence of the last months, and the Bishop's averted head. For now he knew one thing, and knew it well. The lady of his heart lay in that quiet room beyond; and the devils that had fought in him were dead of a Christmas peace.

Little cries came to him, Clo-

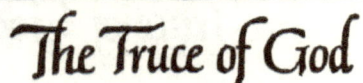

tilde's soft weeping, and another voice that thrilled him, filled with the wooing note that is in a mother's voice when she speaks to her child. But it was a feeble voice, and its weakness struck terror to his soul. What was this thing for which he had cast her away, now that he might lose her? His world shook under his feet. His cousin and enemy was, willy-nilly, become his friend. His world, which he had thought was his own domain, as far from his castle as the eye could reach and as far again, was in an upper room of Philip's house, and dying, perhaps.

But she was not dying. They

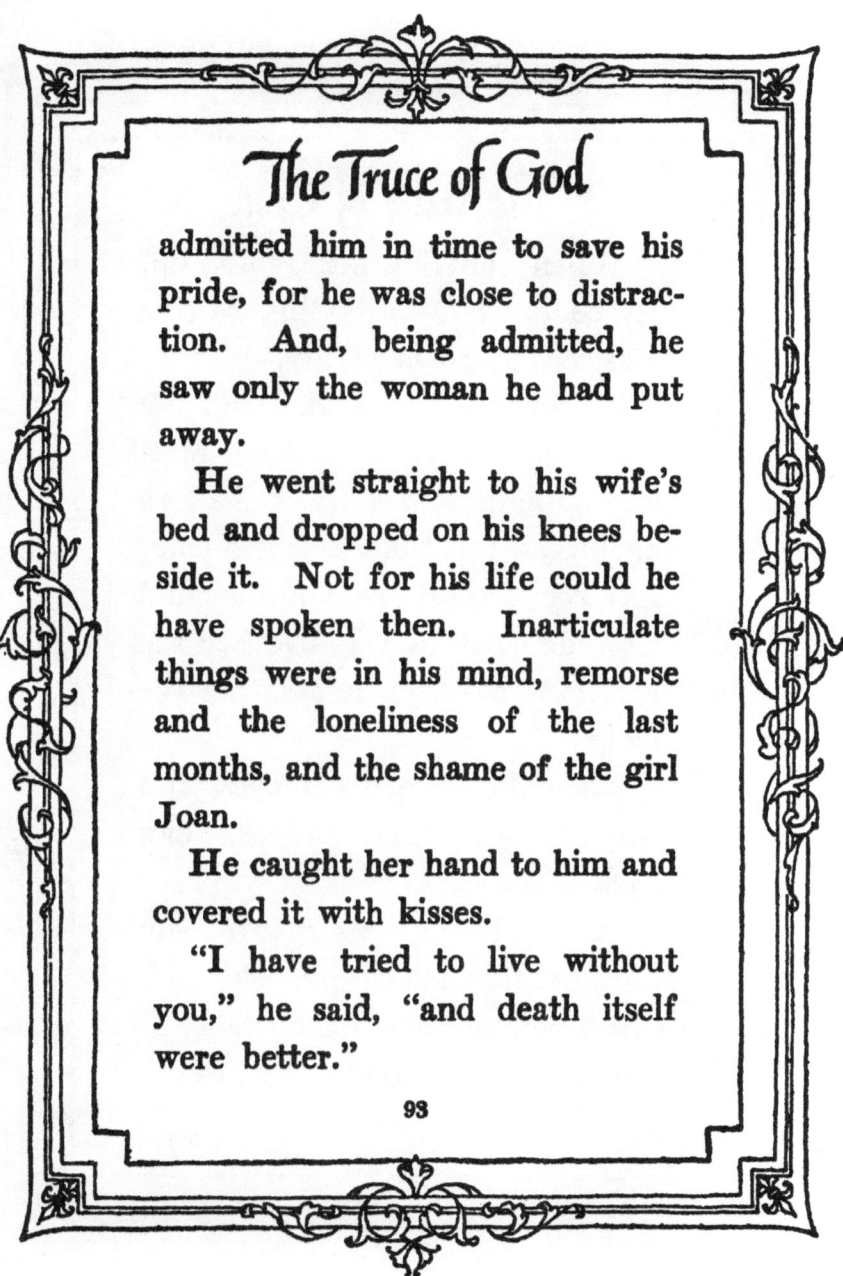

admitted him in time to save his pride, for he was close to distraction. And, being admitted, he saw only the woman he had put away.

He went straight to his wife's bed and dropped on his knees beside it. Not for his life could he have spoken then. Inarticulate things were in his mind, remorse and the loneliness of the last months, and the shame of the girl Joan.

He caught her hand to him and covered it with kisses.

"I have tried to live without you," he said, "and death itself were better."

The Truce of God

When she did not reply, but lay back, white to the lips, he rose and looked down at her.

"I can see," he said, "that my touch is bitterness. I have merited nothing better. So I shall go again, but this time, if it will comfort you, I shall give you the child Clotilde—not that I love her the less, but that you deserve her the more."

Then she opened her eyes, and what he saw there brought him back to his knees with a cry.

"I want only your love, my lord, to make me happy," she said. "And now, see how the birthday of our Lord has brought us peace."

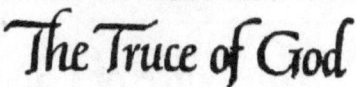

The Truce of God

She drew down the covering a trifle, close to his bent head, and showed the warm curve of her arm. "Unto us also is born a son, Charles."

"I have wanted a son," said Charles the Fair, "but more than a son have I wanted you, heart of my heart."

.   .   .   .

Outside in the courtyard the Fool had drawn a circle about him.

"I am adventuring," he said. "Yesterday I caught this horse when the others ran from him. Then I saved a lady and brought her to her destination. This being

The Truce of God

the Christmas season and a Sunday, I shall rest here for a day." He threw out his chest magnificently. "But tomorrow I continue on my way."

"Can you fight?" They baited him.

"I can sing," he replied. And he threw back his head with its wandering eyes and tender mouth and sang:

"The Light of Light Divine,
True Brightness undefiled.
He bears for us the shame of sin,
A holy, spotless Child."

The End